UTAH'S BEST POETRY & PROSE 2025

SELECTED WINNERS OF THE OLIVE WOOLLEY BURT AND TYPEWRITER AWARDS

CONTENTS

FOREWORD

CASSIDY WARD, 2024 WRITER OF THE YEAR

We humans will find stories in just about anything. We find faces in fleeting wisps of cloud and assign personalities to machines, plants, or weather. We give animals names because some part of us needs to see them as we see ourselves. Maybe it's because we can only truly know ourselves and what drives us, so we must assign to other things, both animate and inanimate, the same motivations.

This all-too-human behavior was clearly demonstrated by a study involving a couple of differently sized triangles, a circle, and a rectangle, carried out by Fritz Heider and Marianne Simmel, psychologists from Austria and Germany respectively, at Smith College in 1944.

Participants were presented with a two-and-a-half-minute stop-motion video in which a small triangle, a large triangle, and a circle moved about the screen. Also present was a hollow rectangle with a section capable of opening in the way a door would.

Despite there being no dialogue, in fact no sound at all, and no emotional cues to inform the viewer's interpretation, Heider and Simmel found that all of the study participants, save one, interpreted the video as having conscious actors.

Upon viewing, they didn't see just two triangles and a circle moving along a nearly empty field. They saw entities with minds. Commonly, they interpreted the triangles as male and the circle as female. They imagined some conflict between the triangles, usually related to some relationship to the circle. In one instance, a participant imagined the large triangle as a mother scolding their children.

The specific interpretations of the video aren't particularly important. What is important is that viewers imbued emotion and complex relationships onto objectively inanimate objects. They filled in the empty cracks with personalities, desires, threats, and injury. They inserted soap opera style drama and resolution. In short, they crafted a story.

The research carried out by Simmel and Heider demonstrated with clarity something each of us likely knows intuitively, something demonstrated by everything we know about our long history. We are a species of storytellers.

There are some pretty obvious ways in which this is true. There are those among us who devote their lives or their free time to writing short stories, novels, television shows, and movies, to crafting songs and comedy specials, to communicating with an audience through the art of narrative in one form or another. You'll find some of them within these pages.

More than that, though, each of us, no matter our vocation, lives a life built on stories. As children, we concoct imaginary friends and exaggerate our real-world experiences to friends on the playground. We daydream, imagining alternate pasts, presents, and futures. We talk to ourselves when we're alone, preparing for situations which may never come to pass, or designing the perfect retort, the thing we wish we would have said in a past argument.

We relate past experiences and amusing or interesting anecdotes around dining room tables, at backyard parties, over the phone, and around campfires. And we dream.

All of these actions, behaviors which comprise a large portion of our waking and sleeping lives, are creative endeavors in the art of fiction. And each time we do this, each time we retell a story or re-imagine a scenario, we refine it. We hone in on the beats, we cut away the fat, we tell the story a little better. We pick up on subtle clues from our audience. We notice the moments they laugh, when their eyes widen, or when attention lags, and we adjust the story. We embellish, rework, and refine.

Storytelling, though, isn't only a social act. It is also deeply personal, an intimate dance which happens inside our individual minds. Each of us has a personal narrative we tell about ourselves, mostly only to ourselves.

As we move through the world, going to school or to work, interacting with friends and family, cashiers and bill collectors, neighbors and strangers, we catalogue those experiences and collate them into a cohesive string of events. It's worth noting that because of the fickle nature of memory, some of the events you hold to be true, maybe even defining events, may not be totally accurate or never happened at all. Even our lives are, to some extent, works of fiction.

The people we encounter become heroes and villains of varying degrees, and always–or at least almost always–we interpret the actions of others and the events we encounter through the lens of how they affect us personally. We are the central character of our own stories.

Humans have been called, among other things, the storytelling animal. From a certain point of view, we can conclude that it isn't our opposable thumbs or our affinity for technology which separates us from the other animals. It is our ability to construct narratives, to define the world and the people in it into settings and characters, which sets us apart.

If Heider and Simmel's research showed us anything, it's that we build stories seemingly without effort. We are, at our most fundamental, machines for building narrative. If triangles and circles moving along an indiscriminate field can become a complex story of love and loss, of conflict and resolution, then anything can. We can't not tell stories. It's the way we communicate with ourselves, the way we reach out to one another, and the way we make sense of an insensible world.

SON OF DEMETER

TYPEWRITER AWARDS, GOLD TYPEWRITER, SHORT FICTION

BRYAN YOUNG

was always told that hypersleep was a blank, black void, absent of everything. I wouldn't think anything, nor would I feel it. I'd wake up as if no time had passed, but fifty years would have gone by. Being a colonist aboard an ark ship was sleepy work.

But I was awake.

I saw nothing, but I felt a lot. And perceived more.

The walls of the pod pressed against me. The tight underclothing we wore pressed tighter than the walls. The scent of chemicals piped into my nostrils with tubes made the whole thing feel clinical, and a still blackness consumed everything.

I tried opening my eyes, though they wouldn't—couldn't—open. But I knew what I would see. Or at least, I assumed I knew. Less than an inch from my face would be the glass window. Someone would be able to look in at me if they were awake and needed to check my vitals. Since I wasn't a member of the crew, I'd be asleep for the entire fifty years, and then I'd be back with my daughter again. Just the two of us against the world, ready to take on anything.

Was I really awake?

Was I dreaming instead?

I tried pinching myself, but my hand didn't respond. I was locked in my coffin-like space so tightly, I couldn't move my hand if I wanted to.

And I wanted to.

Was that something crawling on my arm?

It felt like a spider, each of its eight legs coming up and down along my bicep. It moved upward and forced a chill I didn't know I could experience.

I tried to shoo the spider away, but I was powerless. The phantom spider moved back down my arm with impunity, and I was left to struggle with its tickle against the back of my left hand.

Something must have gone wrong.

Perhaps the chemicals they used to knock us out before the cryo-process had been mixed poorly?

There was no way I was supposed to be conscious..

I wondered what kind of spider it was. Was it something harmless? A daddy long legs? Or was it something much more deadly? A brown recluse? A black widow? Would it bite me? Would I wake in fifty years with a rotted hand from the venom of a long dead spider?

How would a spider even get through the clean area? Foreign objects were strictly forbidden in the hypersleep loading chambers, biological creatures doubly so. It should have been detected on the sensors and vaporized, but the twitch and tickle against my hand said otherwise. There was something in here with me.

Its gnarled teeth plunged into my skin, pumping its venom into my hand. Infecting it.

This was no dream.

I knew that.

The pounding dread ensured that I knew.

But how? Why?

If I were conscious, did that mean my body was aging? My poisoned hand wasn't the only thing that would decay through the journey. In fifty years, they'd pull from my pod a mummified corpse, frozen and dead. Would I starve to death first? How long could I last in a fevered dream like this?

A skitter at my bare feet changed my thoughts. The presence of the spider was gone, replaced by the speed and size of a tiny rodent somewhere down below me. It ran over my toes, and my instinct was to recoil, to flinch and draw my body into itself. To scream.

My god, how I tried to scream.

But like the worst of my nightmares, nothing came out.

And no one knew I was in trouble. No one would ever know.

What had I done to deserve such treatment?

There had to be someone responsible. This doesn't happen on an *Independence*-class colony starship by accident. Unless it always happens and we're all lied to about the nature of hypersleep. Unless this was sabotage.

I wondered where the ship might be on its journey.

Had we left moments ago?

Or would we be arriving imminently?

Were we somewhere in the middle and there were still a couple of decades left?

The rodent stopped its marathon across my feet and finally picked a toe and began to nibble. Its teeth pierced into my small toe first; perhaps that seemed like the easiest target. As much as I wanted to cry out when the spider bit, this was worse, a hundred-fold. Its teeth gnawed nimbly into my flesh, his bones tearing down to mine.

I screamed again.

Or tried.

I was still asleep.

Or half awake.

My mouth wouldn't open; air wouldn't pass through my vocal cords.

The rat cut deeper with its teeth into my phalanges, then deeper, sucking the life from my metatarsals.

I wanted to pity whatever poor soul would be forced to open

my tube and remove my bones, picked clean by the rat, but all I could feel was the pain. It shot like a laser bolt from my foot to my brain, traveling faster than I could comprehend.

Why did someone put such a creature in my pod?

I kicked, or tried to, hoping I could stop the skittering teeth across my skin, sucking the flesh and blood from me. But my leg didn't work.

Defenseless, I tried a different tactic. Dozens of electrodes were attached to my head and my chest. If my mind screamed loud enough, perhaps some passing technician might hear the beeps warning them of abnormal life signs. It was slim hope but better than nothing.

The pain made it easy to conjure the mental energy to scream. The panic that I couldn't give voice to the scream added to my urgency.

I bellowed with my mind, shrieked and screamed with every ounce of energy I could muster.

I felt it in my lungs. Just a bit. As though they knew what they were being called to do, they inflated. But like my voice, they couldn't quite let anything out. My breath stayed there until it slowly trickled away like a pinhole in a boat. A tightness constricted inside me, as if hands were grasping at the lining of my throat.

The rat bit again, slicing into the next toe, ravenously, as though they were long-sought delicacies.

How could I get it out?

How could I end the pain?

I wasn't meant to die like this.

Was I?

Suddenly, the feast of feet stopped, and I knew the pain was so severe that I had numbed myself to it. It was as if my frontal lobe had suffered an overload and shunted the pain away. I'd pay for it later, but for now, my feet were nothing but dead. Maybe the rodent carried on its morbid work, or maybe it didn't. It's not like I could have done anything about it anyway.

I closed my mind's eye, as though that might somehow calm me. A darker blackness shrouded me, and I took in a deep breath —or tried. My lungs still wouldn't respond the way I wanted them to. My deep breath turned into a shallow one, then tighter, as if I were being held underwater.

Drowning.

Dry, in a hypersleep pod, I felt suffocated.

Drowning.

Panic slapped me.

Beat me.

Hit me.

More.

The water level rose.

But then subsided.

I took a breath.

I didn't want to die this way.

Don't.

The water didn't come back.

My breath returned.

I had to think fast.

How could I escape?

I tried mind-screaming once more. I thought I heard a beep, but I needed more than a beep to be more than a blip. I had to do something before the spider-mouse-rat transformed into something else. Something larger. Something deadlier.

This couldn't be normal. There's no way anyone would willingly travel this way if this was what they could expect. That left sabotage. What, or who, would do this to me?

Why would anyone forsake me?

My concentration flagged when I felt something skitter across my cheek and rest on my face just below my eye. Small, clawed feet, sandpaper rough, stopped right there on my crow's feet.

No.

I wished I could wince and tighten my eyes shut to protect them.

Or to shoo away whatever monstrosity stood there over my face.

Because I knew this next part wasn't going to be pleasant.

That's when the claws tightened, bracing themselves for what would happen next. And without a sound, a beak pierced my eyelid and dug into my soft, seeing orb. Still no light or reality penetrated my mind. The blackness grew darker; red bled into it. Sparks came with every peck of the beak.

Something wasn't right.

I wished the sharp beak would pierce further into my eye, through it, into my brain, and peck away at it, tearing up shreds of it and eating them, just so it would end the pain. There was nothing that made me want to continue living in this dark limbo of pain and torture.

Perhaps it was poison, I wondered, as the beak sheared again into my face. I heard the slurping crack as it broke the bone around my eye socket. The pain didn't even faze me anymore. It was just a part of this existence.

Once, twice, thrice the beak came down. It didn't feel like anything but pressure against my face—someone, or something, pressing the edge of a knife against my eye and feeling it press into my head and brain.

Plenty of biological agents could provide effects like these.

Because there was no way this could have been real. Had my hand really been gnarled with venom? My toes gnawed off by vermin? My eyes pecked out by a monster?

Why was I still alive? How could I be if it were real?

It was real enough.

Focus determines reality, and all I could focus on was the horror.

The despair.

The pain.

Years passed, or at least what felt like years. Pain came and went. It manifested itself in different ways. Spiders, sometimes, crawling across my body. Stings of scorpions at my feet. A clawed monster scooping out the contents of my chest to eat like so much bloody ice cream. I don't even want to mention what the centipedes crawling into my ears felt like or the maggots dissolving my groin.

And more years passed this way.

Finally, light pierced my gaze. Bright, white light. It hurt almost as much as the torture, blinding. But sounds returned. Sounds of activity filled my ears like the centipedes had, but for the first time, the sounds weren't coming from inside my own head.

"Wha…?" My mouth worked. My voice. I could scream again if I needed or wanted to. Or at least I felt like I could.

I shut my eyes tighter against the onslaught of light, convinced this was another trick. The blinding light was just another way to torture me, to force me to live my eternity in constant fear. They had changed their tactics over many years, so why wouldn't this be some new technique in the arsenal of my pain?

"Get him to the medcenter," a voice said.

I still couldn't make out shapes or colors. Every time I tried to crack my eyes open, I had to seal them back up for fear of being blinded by the intensity of light, like I was staring at a cold sun.

Was this all real? If I really was going to the medcenter… How bad was the damage? Was I a decimated corpse? An emaciated skeleton picked through with just enough vitality to keep alive after such an ordeal? I couldn't feel my flesh. My skin felt outside of me. I wore it as a jacket, and my bones slid underneath it.

I couldn't even remember what the medcenter looked like or how far it was from the time I'd been put down.

Down.

Out.

Hands on me, at my shoulders and legs. They maneuvered me around and laid me down on something.

I bobbed up and down as we went.

A stretcher?

I didn't want to get my hopes up. Life had become nothing but pain. Why would this be any different?

The bobbing stopped, and I was tossed like refuse onto a bed.

"Whhha… whe… ho…" I could make sounds, but they didn't mean anything. I couldn't ask questions. I couldn't communicate.

Another nightmare.

I'd been given a voice but was unable to use it properly.

"Don't speak," a voice said.

Hands gripped my arm—the one that had been bloated and killed by a spider's bite. They turned and twisted it, tapping it for something. Then, a needle plunged into my arm. It bit me, and I wanted to twist and shout and scream, but I had no strength to resist. My arms flopped, which was more than they'd been able to do in a hundred years. My dusty voice tried resisting but coughed sand.

A moment passed.

Then another.

And I expected the needle digging into the center of my dead arm to explode or rot away from the final poison they were injecting into me.

Instead, a warmth grew from the epicenter. It radiated outward.

Medcenter.

Medicine.

How were they turning this against me?

How would this end in pain?

In my mind, I was black and white, a skeleton, dead. Death and life at once. But as the elixir of life pumped from their machine into my veins, it radiated color outward, bringing me back to my normal state. It fed up my arm and reached my heart with a warmth I hadn't known in a lifetime. My heart worked overtime, nothing more than a machine pumping medicine to tainted blood.

One by one, life returned to my limbs, first one leg, then another. My toes wiggled, uneaten.

When the warmth of a fireplace on a winter's day reached my head and my eyes, I dared to try opening them again. The light was bright but not blindingly so. I peeked, hoping to see what there was to see.

Three technicians stood over me.

The first people I'd seen in an eternity. Since I was knocked out. Chewed up. Spit out.

"Doctor…?" I asked.

But no one responded.

One of them brought out a pen. They clicked it, and a light appeared at the end. With rubber-gloved hands, she pulled my eye open and pressed the light near me, blinding me again.

Examining.

Exploring.

Wondering.

Diagnosing.

"And the test?" one said.

"Negative," another responded.

"As I thought," the third stated.

But what test? Was that all this was? They'd put me through this as a test?

I growled, angry.

I didn't like being a guinea pig.

Hadn't they done enough to me?

They left the room. At least, I think they left the room. The bright lights turned to blackness again, and I must have drifted back into sleep.

I didn't want to sleep anymore. I'd been asleep for what felt like a thousand years. I didn't want to go back to that place. Sleep was where hurt came. Where I was defenseless. But I couldn't help but surrender to the color radiating from my arm.

I woke up screaming.

I don't know how long I was out, but the second I was conscious enough to stop sleeping, I did.

The lights in the room were dim already but brightened

slightly when I woke. An alarm sounded. Not the sort of banshee shrieks and daemonic klaxons I expected after my ordeal, but a subdued pinging. Nurses entered the room. Three of them.

Two came to my side and did their best to lay me back. The third went to the bag above my head and started to inject something. "No… Don't…"

"Sir, please," one nurse said.

But the other ignored them both. "Get him back down. He's in no state—"

"No!" I roared, shoving one away from me.

But I was nothing more than a paper tiger. I'd not really gotten a good look at myself, and seeing my arms flail, I realized I was loose skin wrapped around bones. Had the nurses been children, I still wouldn't have been able to fend them off.

Their concoction hit the IV, and I was sedated again. Drifting off toward pain. And sleep.

I heard them talking in my hazy stupor.

Words I didn't quite understand.

"Affected."

"Apologies."

"Aggravate."

Who was apologizing? What was happening? I was definitely affected, but by what? I was definitely aggravated.

Though I fought against it, trying to think through what was happening, sleep took me again. I couldn't fight very hard against anything.

I woke again.

Less screaming.

Less panic.

They must have put something in that cocktail dangling above me to keep me sedated because I wanted to worry. I just couldn't muster the energy. Or maybe I was just tired.

Then sleep took me once more.

I didn't struggle against it so hard this time.

It felt more peaceful.

Restful.

Easy.

"Wake up, Mr. Garcia," a voice said through the void.

I hadn't had a voice do that before. In my decades of torture, the only discernible voice I heard was my own.

"Mr. Garcia," the voice said again. "Please, wake up."

My eyes fluttered easily, taking in the bright light around me. I flinched, but only barely.

"Where am I?" I asked, my voice dragged across broken glass to speak.

I could see I was in a hospital room of some type with silver bulkhead walls and no windows. There was a doctor, or someone I presumed to be a doctor, in front of me. She looked groggy, as though she'd been woken up early, too.

"You're in the infirmary, Mr. Garcia. And I'm Dr. Broadnax."

"You're who?" Speaking was difficult, and it hurt, but it hurt more to be silenced.

"Dr. Broadnax. We need to discuss your options."

"Options?"

"Yes. Well, you see, you're in a very unusual situation."

"Someone… was trying to kill me," I said.

She smiled. "About that… That's what we need to talk to you about."

"Yes, I want to… press charges…"

"Well, it's…" The doctor took a breath. Unsure of how to speak, of what to say. She looked to the side and scrunched her nose in thought. Then, the words came to her. "Why don't we start with where you are, shall we?"

"Okay."

"You're aboard the Space-Ark Demeter."

"Yes…"

"And we're currently about three hundred thousand miles from Earth."

"From… Earth?"

"Yes, we've just broken lunar orbit for our first slingshot into the stars."

"But that means…"

"Yes. We're only a few days into our fifty year voyage."

I gasped. I'd been tortured for centuries. At the very least, I hoped I'd just wake up in my new home, the agony would be over, and I'd never have to endure such a thing again.

"So, this is why we need to talk about choices. You see, we ran some tests and discovered that your psychometric and biological profiles had an error in them. We ran some tests, and we've found that you're mildly allergic to the agents used to induce hypersleep comas."

"Mildly?"

"Yes. Despite your elevated vital signs and internal perception, you're no worse for wear. So, we have two options."

Bile filled my stomach and threatened to erupt.

"What about my daughter? Is she like this, too?"

The doctor flipped through a few screens on her pad and continued confidently, "We've monitored her since your tests came back. She's had no signs of these effects and is hibernating normally. Though allergies can be genetic, she doesn't seem to share this one."

I covered my mouth with my hand. The only thing worse than enduring a lifetime of this agony was thinking my daughter would have to as well. My voice grew hoarse, and my vision blurred with tears. "What are the options?"

The doctor took in a sharp breath. "We can put you back to sleep and you can endure the rest of the journey as you have been so far. When you wake, you'll be reunited with your daughter. We're wary of that option, though. The psychological stress might be irreversible after a week, let alone fifty years."

The blood drained from my face, and I felt like I would pass out considering such a thing. "And the other?"

"The other option is that you can live out your remaining days here aboard the Demeter. We can look into resynthesizing the coma agent in a way you're not allergic to, but I'll be frank: the chances aren't good for that, given our limited medical capabilities and access to new materials here on the ship."

My future flashed before my eyes. Growing old aboard a starship. What would that look like? Would I become a burden? How would I deal with social interaction? The ship rotated its crew every year. I'd be saying goodbye to everyone I'd ever known with an alarming regularity. The next time they'd see me would be during their second rotation twenty-five years later.

And I'd have already said goodbye to my daughter for the last time.

Or I could endure torture? A hundred thousand years of mind-numbing, mind-destroying agony just to see her smile once more.

"Can't you just turn around? Send us back? We're still close to Earth…"

"Unfortunately, we've already begun our slingshot maneuver. The window for aborting the mission has closed. I'm sorry."

I had to make a choice.

It was really no choice at all.

I looked down at my hand, which seemed much more solid than it had the last time I had fallen asleep. Even wasting away had been an illusion of the drugs. "My name is Santiago Garcia, Doctor," I said, trying not to cry while extending my hand to shake hers. "And I'd like you to put me back to sleep…"

WATER HEMLOCK

OLIVE WOOLLEY BURT AWARDS, HONORABLE MENTION, POETRY: HAIKU

C. H. LINDSAY

water hemlock blooms
along marshes and rivers—
fragrant death awaits

WHERE THERE'S A WILL, THERE'S A WISP

OLIVE WOOLLEY BURT AWARDS, FIRST PLACE, SCIENCE FICTION & FANTASY

C.W. ALLEN

ots of birds whistle. That part wasn't strange. But to Myron, this one sounded… well, almost human.

No, not human. More like a cartoon. The sort of whistle used as wordless, semi-musical shorthand for "look over here." In old cartoons, people usually had to stick their fingers in their mouths to make that sound.

Birds don't have fingers.

It was a small, unremarkable bird. Just a feathery little blob, six different shades of brown, like an ordinary sparrow. The kind that congregates in neglected parking lots, bathing in puddles and searching for dropped bits of corn chips or french fries. True to form, this was an urban bird, strutting between the gutter and the shop fronts lining the Main Street walkway. But this one was alone. And it wouldn't stop *staring* at him.

The bird did a jaunty little hop down the sidewalk then turned and looked back at Myron, waiting. When he closed the distance, only three steps away, the bird hopped along again.

Hop-hop-hop. Turn. Wait. Hop-hop-hop. Turn. Wait.

When the bird hop-hop-hopped its way down an alley, Myron made a brief experiment—he continued strolling casually along the sidewalk, careful not to glance down the alley as he passed it.

Just as he suspected, the bird whistled at him again, and when that didn't slow him down, it flew past and fluttered to a stop at his feet.

He must have imagined the glare and the exasperated sigh.

Myron raised his palms in defense. "All right! Whatever you say, boss. Where are we going?"

Down a grimy brick alley, apparently, past broken bottles and the windswept remains of plastic bags, to a weathered wooden door.

The bird bobbed onto the threshold and pecked at the door's flaking purple paint. *TAP-ta-tap-tappity-TAP.* (Myron could have sworn it sounded like a secret knock.)

A brass mail slot, set at eyeball height, clanged open. "Yes?" said a cautious voice from the other side.

Myron's gaze flicked down to the doorstep, as though he expected the bird to finally explain the nature of their errand. But the bird was gone.

"This is going to sound—" Myron began. But before he could blather any further, he was interrupted by the hollow *thunk* of the door unbolting, and a middle-aged woman ushered him into a small, shabby waiting room.

"If you don't think I'll believe what led you here," she said, "then you're definitely in the right place."

The "right place" was, to Myron's eye… some kind of shop? A mismatched jumble of seats lined the walls: stuffy wingback armchairs, tall metal stools, worn wooden chairs borrowed from a dozen different dining tables. The far wall, facing the sidewalk, was made entirely of frosted glass. Where the shop's front door should have been, an outline of a door had been painted onto the glass, complete with letters stenciled backwards so they could be read from the street—CLOSED. A red velvet curtain hung from the ceiling between two of the chairs, concealing whatever lay beyond this waiting room.

They looked each other up and down. Myron peered quizzically at the woman's frazzled salt-and-pepper curls and rustic leather work apron. Jeweled spectacles perched at the end of her stubby nose, secured around her neck with a length of gold filigree chain. The top of her head only reached the middle of his chest. He couldn't decide if she reminded him more of a fussy librarian or a gruff blacksmith. (Blacksmith? Why did that word pop into his head? There were no blacksmiths in the city. Or in this century, for that matter.) The woman returned his skeptical inspection, frowning at Myron's frayed jeans and tattered sneakers, his mussed mouse-brown hair and a chin's worth of day-old stubble.

"You'll do," she announced at last.

"*Do?* Do what?"

"As my new apprentice, of course. Isn't that why you're here?"

Myron didn't have a clue as to why he was there. He tried to explain about the bird, and the whistling, and the hopping. He'd been minding his own business, just running errands. But the bird wouldn't leave him in peace.

A wry smile twisted the woman's lips. "Peace? You were at peace, then, before the bird ruined everything?"

Myron's gaze fell to his shoelaces. He didn't have to part with the details—reduced hours at his mind-numbing job, electric company threatening to cut him off, apartment building clearing all the tenants out for a year-long renovation into condos none of them could hope to afford. His weary expression told a truer story than words could have managed. He mumbled something about being on his way to the temp agency when he heard the whistling.

The woman nodded sagely. "It's quite rare, you know."

Myron argued that it seemed like a perfectly ordinary bird to him. But for some reason, this sent the woman laughing.

"Not the bird, dear boy—you! It's not every day you meet a young man whose ear is tuned to hear the call of the whip-poor-will-o-the-wisp."

"I—what?"

"You've heard of will-o-the-wisps, yes? Mysterious lights in swamps and forests, leading travelers to their fates?"

Myron thought he recalled stories where the lights lured travelers to unexpected doom, but when he brought this up, the woman dismissed the notion as superstitious hogwash. The wisps served Fate, she insisted. Whether one's fate was welcome was a matter of opinion.

"We couldn't very well expect wisps to float around the city," she went on. "Electric lights interfere. No one would notice them. But birds make their homes wherever they find themselves, cities included. And whip-poor-wills in particular have a knack for drawing attention with their distinctive whistling. It was only natural they'd fill an empty niche and put themselves at Fate's service."

"So, the bird…" Myron paused as the thought collected itself on his tongue. "It decided I needed to work… wherever this is?"

"I don't know how much say the bird had in the matter. More of a messenger, really. But you chose to listen. If you'd insisted on carrying about your errands, the bird couldn't have stopped you. Might have aimed a well-timed splatter to express its annoyance at being ignored, but then that would have been Fate too."

The woman still hadn't explained what sort of work she was hiring for, or even introduced herself, for that matter. But since Myron had been on his way to a job interview anyway, he decided there was no point wasting this one. He offered the woman his name and a handshake, hoping that might nudge more information out of her.

"Lyra." She gripped his hand with a firm intensity he hadn't expected from someone practically half his height and at least twice his age. Then, she held the velvet curtain aside and waved him through.

The room beyond the curtain was as busy as the entryway was bare. One entire wall was a bubblegum-pink pegboard, meticulously organized with every sort of tool imaginable (and several Myron couldn't have imagined.) Delicate jeweler's tweezers in sizes from tiny to miniscule waited on the pegboard's hooks next to a massive sledgehammer, a set of woodworking chisels, a hand crank eggbeater, and something that looked like cross between a monkey wrench and an octopus. The next wall was a cubby system that looked like it might have come from IKEA… if IKEA were run by giant bees. Interlocking hexagons made of sleek white resin, stacked from floor to ceiling, held jars of assorted buttons, pots of wax, glue, polish, and lacquer, paintbrushes of all sizes, and skeins of yarn in colors Myron didn't know existed. The next wall was lined with rustic wooden barrels, stamped across the front with red lettering: MOONDUST, ASSORTED WISH-BONES, POWDERED DIAMONDS, SOAP. A wrought-iron spiral staircase occupied the far corner, and the center of the room was one massive square work table scattered with a strange assortment of damaged items: a ceramic figurine of a mermaid that was missing its left tail fin, a deck of tattered playing cards, a tarnished silver flute, and a Persian rug caked with globs of dried mud.

"So, what do you think?" asked Lyra.

"Nice, uh… repair shop?" Myron guessed.

Apparently, his answer was satisfactory. Lyra nodded and gestured him toward a pair of rolling stools stationed at the work-table. "You look like you could use a cup of tea."

Myron thanked her and lowered his lanky frame onto one of the stools. Lyra bustled over to a utility sink under the staircase and filled a kettle then pulled an electric hotplate from one of the bee cubbies to start it heating.

"You've noticed, I take it, that this isn't a typical repair shop?" Lyra ventured as she took her seat at the table.

"I couldn't exactly miss it," said Myron, thinking of the feathered recruiter and the false entrance.

"You definitely *could,*" Lyra insisted. "Most people do. They see what they expect to see. Anything that doesn't tally with their understanding of the world, they're more than eager to ignore. But *you,*" she added, wagging a finger at him, "you were actually looking. And unbiased observation happens to be the only skill that matters in this business. I can teach you all the rest."

"Teach me what, exactly?"

Lyra waved a dismissive hand. "Oh, you know. Polishing a djinn's bottle or an enchanted mirror without offending the spirits inside. Rebinding old spellbooks. Getting stains out of a flying carpet. That sort of thing."

Myron pointed to the rug sprawled across the far corner of the worktable. "You're telling me *that's* a flying carpet?"

"Well, not in this condition, it's not. Just look at it! Absolutely filthy. It can't even hover, let alone make it above the cloud line for a long journey. But with a bit of shampoo and elbow grease…" She peered at Myron over the top of her glasses. When he didn't laugh or storm out, she continued.

"There's no magic in the work, you know. It's just mending and polishing, a little glue and paint here, stitching up a few loose threads there. But our clients can't entrust their items to a run-of-the-mill dry cleaner or tailor. I mean, can you imagine an ordinary cobbler trying to resole enchanted dancing shoes?"

"I thought you said everyone ignores the stuff they don't expect," Myron reminded her.

Lyra arched a dubious eyebrow at him. "A painted-on shop door is one thing. You'd have to be delusional to tune out a pair of cowboy boots doing the can-can across your workshop."

The debate was interrupted by the teakettle's whistle. Lyra returned to the cabinet by the sink, but this time, she didn't bustle. She stretched out the moment, carefully measuring a precise spoonful of sugar into each of the mismatched mugs, considering her collection of antique storage tins, finally selecting the speckled blue one and popping off the lid. She scooped out its contents into the plain porcelain teapot. All the while the kettle sang from the hotplate. Only when every other task was complete did she finally empty the kettle into the teapot so the leaves could start soaking.

"Let me help." Myron jumped up to ferry the teapot and one of the mugs back to the worktable.

Lyra followed, clutching her own mug and nursing a secretive smile.

The tea and conversation brewed. Myron groused about his

job and housing search, lamenting the city's skyrocketing rent prices. Lyra dropped a casual reference to the shop's vacant upstairs apartment into her anecdote about renovating a set of haunted bagpipes.

When Myron poured their tea, Lyra didn't drink hers right away. She stared intently at Myron through the cloud of perfumed steam wafting from her mug.

"So, what do you think?"

It was the second time she had asked that question but the first time he'd truly considered it. Myron was silent for a moment, gazing thoughtfully around the workshop. He blew gently on his mug and took a slow sip. "Frère Jacques," he said at last.

"Pardon?"

"Frère Jacques," Myron repeated. "Your tea kettle was whistling the tune. But the last note is a bit off. Really flat, actually."

"You don't say?" A sly sideways grin drifted across Lyra's face. "Clever of you to notice. I'll have to look into that."

"Might just need a good cleaning," Myron suggested. "I suspect all that boiling water causes some mineral scaling."

Lyra took a slow sip of her own. "What makes you think so?"

Myron stood, rolled up his sleeves, and headed for the sink. "I don't think I mentioned my résumé," he called over his shoulder as he searched the cabinet for some dish soap and a rag. "It's been a few years, but my first job was in the kitchen of this fancy Italian restaurant. Never did learn to cook anything, but I must have scrubbed their pasta pots thousands of times. I can get your kettle sorted out in no time."

Lyra chuckled into her mug. "I'm sure you will."

———

The sink trickled. Lyra sipped. Myron scrubbed.

He still wasn't sure about this Fate business. Or the bird. But Lyra had insisted both left the choice up to him. And something about that—not just accepting his fate but *choosing* it—made all the morning's oddness melt away. Maybe it was time to focus less on what sort of work he wanted to do and more on how he wanted to feel while doing it.

There was a kind of beauty—simplicity, really—in restoring old things instead of discarding them. And power, too, in the way ordinary care and precision could make a broken item extraordinary again. He knew it was silly to think of objects in such personal terms. But then, he'd had plenty of experience feeling broken and discarded himself. Suddenly, the idea of a repair shop felt less like work and more like a devotion.

He'd never really cared about anything on that level. He'd never had anything worth caring about. Or caring *for*.

Myron kept on scrubbing, but now he carried a secret smile of his own. He barely even noticed when he began to whistle.

TRUST NO ONE

TYPEWRITER AWARDS, SILVER TYPEWRITER, NONFICTION

CAROLYN CAMPBELL

than Parker is only one of his fake names. He looks like a kid that might mow your neighbor's lawn or take your sister to the prom. You wouldn't be a bit scared if Parker stood in line behind you at the bank. Nothing about his blond good guy looks reveals the terror he brought to an estimated fifty victims. He didn't break into anyone's home using lock picks or a crowbar. Instead, his pure evil invaded their safety via Snapchat or other online platforms. Even then, his white-meat Mormon boy appearance didn't cause the fear that led one victim to hide in her bathroom for an hour after they chatted online. Parker's terrifying threats seemed far removed from the South Jordan home where he lived with his parents. And while he showed his victims he knew where they lived and threatened everything from rape to human trafficking, he didn't even ask for money. "He was a shock to the Utah system, says Sarah Lundquist, the Special Agent and investigator for the ICAC (Internet Crimes Against Children) Task Force who investigated Ethan Parker.

Lundquist discovered Parker's multiple online accounts. She preserved data in preparation for writing search warrants. "I would hold the data and then write warrants for all the accounts," she says. She continues, "The nature of Snapchat is to hide, be secretive, and disappear instantly. It's all about anonymity and being naughty online." Because of its instantaneous nature, most Snapchat users don't save much stuff—but Parker did. "He saved so much content that I couldn't read it all. It was good for us, bad for him," she adds. Parker used another application designed specifically for teens. Through understanding this app, Lundquist realized, "You had to ensure you were a teen to get on this app. Users put their social media handles there." When Parker contacted a female teen, the conversation would start innocently for a couple of weeks or months. By then, he often had the girl's photo from her accounts.

Then, the conversational tone changed. "Tbh, I'm horny asf. Would you be willing to help me out?" he asked one victim. She said no. He replied, "Help, or I will expose you. You have one minute to send a bra pic." She declined again. He said, "You have one minute to send a nude boobs pic, or I will expose you."

"How will you expose me?" the girl asked.

"If you don't send me what I want, I will photoshop your face onto naked photos and send them out to all your friends and family," he replied.

Lundquist explains, "With Snapchat, if your location is on, anybody can see it, down to the exact home or business where you are." Parker took screenshots of his victims' locations. When one said she wasn't scared and refused his demands, he sent four screenshots of her home. "He would Zoom out and then slowly zoom in to the victim's house and say, "I will send rapists and human traffickers to your house." At times, he threatened to visit the victim's home and rape her himself. Or he said he would send "all the creeps I can find online." Says Lundquist, "His threats would scare an adult, let alone a kid who can't see past her phone."

Ethan Parker, the abovementioned predator, and Matt Morgan, a victim of a different predator, are two sides of the same deadly coin. Both fair-haired and youthful, their similar appearance suggests they could be high school classmates. In high school, Morgan played two varsity sports, sang in choirs, and was an honor student with college plans. In an out-of-character move, he sent a sexually explicit video to someone he met online. Threats and terror started. A single phone number texted him more than a thousand times—sometimes every thirty seconds. He sent all the money he had ever saved or earned to the entity that tormented him. His final message begged, "Please don't do this. You just killed a 16-year-old kid." Moments later, he died by suicide.

"He was a good kid—one I won't forget, says John Peirce, a Davis County Sheriff's detective who investigated Morgan's case. To help assure peace for Morgan's family, Peirce requested that his real name not be used. Within Peirce's investigative work, he's aware of at least six other suicides following sextortion. Many such cases follow a typical scenario where, as soon as the online friend receives the illicit photo, seemingly unstoppable money demands begin. Sometimes, perpetrators post photos even after being paid. All agencies interviewed for this article say that sextortion perpetrated against male victims has increased dramatically during the last two to three years. "Boys are the big ones when it comes to money. Someone online will kind of catfish the victim, showing interest and pretending to be someone his age," said Matt Thompson, Assistant ICAC (Internet Crimes Against Children) Commander. "They submit images they find online and try to get the child to be comfortable and submit similar images back. One of the first things they sometimes do is ask for the passwords to the kid's account. Then they can go in and see their contacts. The victim is vulnerable at that point." The groomer goes on their Facebook or Snapchat and friends one of their friends, saying, "I know Sara. Can I be your friend, too?" While some groomers look for marginalized kids, others pursue outgoing, popular kids who feel they have much to lose. "Our cyber tips started coming in exponentially during COVID. COVID could be where the increase started because everybody was at home online."

Sgt. Bob Scott of the Unified Police Department Special Victims Unit explains that Morgan and Parker's stories are examples of the two most common types of sextortion he sees. In the first type, the victim is male, most likely from thirteen to eighteen years old. He chats with someone he meets online but doesn't know personally. The perpetrator assumes the persona of an attractive girl. "The conversation goes in a sexual direction. She asks him to go to another type of app—Instant Messenger, Instagram, Snapchat, or Discord. He's given a link," Scott explains. His online acquaintance, who he still assumes is a real-live girl, says, "If you send me nude pictures of you, I will send you naked photos of me." The request might include masturbation videos. "While this video is being recorded, something will come up, and she'll say, 'talk to you later,'" says Scott. He adds, "As soon as the individual gets what they need, the calls become threatening with statements such as, 'We have your naked photos. We will send them to all of your family and friends and the authorities unless you pay us.'" Thompson recalls a sextortion that occurred practically overnight with a teenage victim in Silicon Valley who was considered popular and a good kid with a college scholarship. He complied with a demand to send illicit images. Then, he took his phone to bed with him at 10:00 p.m. After the sextortionist emailed him a picture, he thought his life was over and hanged himself at 4:00 a.m. "In this type of sextortion, the goal is to pursue money and fraud," says Scott.

While perpetrators seek money in the first sextortion type, in the second, victims are female, and perpetrators seek photos. In a typical picture-for-picture exchange. "The grooming can take months before they ask for nude photos," says Scott. Before reaching out, the perpetrator might compile a sort of dossier— where the victim lives, works, her likes and dislikes. Lundquist says one of her biggest takeaways from investigating Parker's case is, "On the internet, you never know what tiny amount of information will help someone find you. You go to this high school. You went to this funeral." Adds Scott, "Once they receive the first nude photos, they ask for more—possibly videos and all kinds of illicit things."' This second type of sextortion isn't financially motivated, but should it accelerate, the perpetrator might want to meet the victim and even kidnap her.

Parker found girls' photos on other platforms or their own accounts. He made some victims supply other usernames. When he threatened to post pictures, "Some would fight him and say, 'Go ahead and do it.'" says Lundquist. "Some tried to sound tough because they were scared to death." She adds that a New York police officer's daughter sent Parker a photo of a bible. She wrote, "Good luck with that on Photoshop."

Lundquist's investigation into Ethan Parker led to a middle-class South Jordan house. Rather than issuing a warrant, she pursued a "knock and talk," knocking on the potential suspect's door at home. After a woman answered, Lundquist asked, "May I speak to your son?" The woman replied, "He's not here." Lundquist asked, "When will he be back?" The woman shook her head. "Not for a long time. He's serving an LDS mission in Mexico." Was this missionary her suspect? Lundquist wasn't sure yet. Continuing to search, she discovered that the innocent-looking former Bingham High School student and current missionary was, indeed, Ethan Parker. Only his real name was Gabe Gilbert. An LDS church attorney spoke with Lundquist. He told her that Gilbert's mother had contacted his mission president. After the president interviewed Gilbert, the church quickly sent him home. Lundquist commends the LDS Church for their handling of the situation. "They didn't know [about his online activities] until they knew, then they sent him home right away."

While Gilbert's missionary status may have shocked Utah, Lundquist explains that she has arrested people from all walks of life. "With any suspect, there is a sense of disappointment, frustration, and anger, but no more so than when we find newly identified victims, such as in this case. While we need to maintain control of our emotions to do this work, I have sometimes absolutely cried for the victims."

City Weekly approached two victims' families to seek their insights. Morgan's family and Jessica's (not her real name), a girl Gilbert victimized, declined to be interviewed. Gilbert approached Jessica to submit illicit photos. She refused and never sent pictures. Her father says, "I'm proud of her for standing up to this guy instead of giving in to the threats. If more victims did that and spoke out about it, these predators might think twice about their actions." Declining City Weekly's interview request, he said, "I'd tell the reporter that this stuff has lasting effects on the victims whether they send pictures or not. I'm glad this guy is in prison. I have no sympathy for him."

Lundquist adds, "It should be emphasized that [sextortion] is traumatizing; you now have two families who do not want to speak about it because it is very triggering." While declining an interview, Jessica helped Lundquist's investigation by identifying a half-face photo of Gilbert.

A Texas Snapchat user initially reported Gilbert to NCMEC— the National Center for Missing and Exploited Children. Their staff studied the identifiers—IP addresses, phone numbers, and geolocation. Identifiers told them to submit the case to the Utah ICAC office. Seeing the rising sextortion trend, the Utah ICAC office started counting in April and received seventy-four cyber tips by August. "These can be from the child victim or their parents," says Thompson. He explains that the Utah Attorney General's Office oversees ICAC. The Department of Justice wanted to assemble a program of task forces nationwide to prevent Internet crimes and sexual exploitation against children. "For twenty-one years, we have had a federal grant for ICAC and received state money through the legislature to help fund this program. It covers the entire state for agencies willing to come on board and let us train them in protecting kids."

Sextortion has several varieties. Aside from the situations such as Morgan's and Gilbert's, "There are domestic situations where adults or minors who were once in an intimate relationship and have intimate images of each other want to use that against each other at some point, for some kind of gain or emotional abuse." ICAC investigated one man who police later arrested on a "human trafficking type charge." Like Morgan and Gilbert, he outwardly "looked like he was an average, decent person," says Thompson. "A well-to-do local businessman. We discovered he had solicited and paid dozens of kids in Utah and other states for sending him illicit content. He didn't sell or share any of it. It was all content for his personal use," says Thompson.

After she knew Gilbert was home from his mission, Lundquist went to his home to try to speak with him. His family declined her request. Once Gilbert's family retained an attorney, "They made it clear he wasn't going to make a statement," says Lundquist. Gilbert's parents knew nothing of his sextortion activities before his arrest. The young man, who appeared to "check all the boxes" by attending Bingham High School and serving a mission, was now in court. In 3rd District Court, Gilbert was charged with five counts of aggravated sexual extortion of a child, a first-degree felony, and four counts of sexual exploitation of a minor, a second-degree felony. Court records state that, as part of a plea agreement, in exchange for the guilty pleas, they recommended that: "a maximum sentence of five years will be a just sentence in this matter." Lundquist said, "He pled guilty to all nine charges. His attorney arranged for him to surrender himself at our office." She never heard Gilbert speak, "not even in the car on the way to the jail," she recalls. While they never spoke, Lundquist recalls questions she would like to ask Gilbert. "I wanted to know why he chose the means he did," she says. She imagined she might say, "In the life you were living, how did your addiction become so bad that you need to send rapists and human traffickers to girls' houses to get what you want when it is so readily available online?"

The person who sextorted Morgan was believed to be located on the African Ivory Coast. Thompson explains that sextortionists from there, Nigeria, and the Philippines, "are good at manipulating kids. They threaten to expose them to all their friends, grandma, and parents." Do sextortionists work together in call centers there? "I don't have firsthand knowledge of it [call centers], but the volume of cases originating from that part of the world certainly suggests there is some sort of organized criminal effort." How do teenagers get money to pay? "You would be surprised how many kids have Venmo," says Thompson.

In foreign cases, law enforcement often works with Homeland Security. Although the county attorney planned to prosecute Morgan's perpetrator and the regional embassy offered support, investigators couldn't determine the suspect's identity or location with no IP address. Peirce says it was also determined that no one would extradite the suspect. This incomplete ending is a typical result following sextortion from Nigeria and the Ivory Coast. "It's not like don't try—the case gets out of our hands here," says Thompson.

Like Morgan and Gilbert, future victims will likely appear to be ordinary kids walking home from school or playing video games. And that's who they'll be—everyday kids spending time online. How can they avoid becoming sextortion victims?

They can realize that social media is full of predatory individuals, says Scott. "Don't allow friend requests from people you don't know. Don't share intimate photos even if you know the other person," he continues, "Never send money. If you send a hundred dollars, they will ask for two hundred." If sextortion happens to you, realize you aren't alone, and it isn't your fault. "It doesn't matter what happened. If you have been a victim, please tell someone—a parent, coach, mentor, or religious leader who can help guide you." He adds, "You made a mistake. You aren't a criminal."

Thompson advises parents to know their kids well enough to have age-appropriate conversations about online safety. "It's terrifying, especially for a kid who thinks. 'Holy crap, what am I going to do?'" He and other law enforcement officials interviewed for this article plan to increase awareness by making presentations statewide and investigating more cases. "Anyone who wants to exploit a kid, we will go after," Thompson says. "If they go after a child, they will hurt anybody."

Previously published in Salt Lake City Weekly

A WISH COME TRUE

OLIVE WOOLLEY BURT AWARDS, FIRST
PLACE, POETRY: LIGHT VERSE

D.J. WRAY

Marvin Melville was a jovial chap,
who lived by the seat of his pants.
Having gone bald at a rather young age,
he'd amassed quite a collection of hats.
Passing a mirror was tedious
as he could not overlook his bald pate.
Wishing one night, on the first evening star,
he prayed to change this state.
"Star light, star bright," he whispered
as he scrunched his eyes up tight.
"I wish I may, oh, how I wish I might
have the wish I wish tonight."
Imagining himself with long, flowing locks,
Marvin crossed his fingers for extra oomph.
Again, picturing lustrous hair,
he didn't think about limiting the length.
Throw into the mix his lucky rabbit's foot,
four leaf clover, and horseshoe, end-up.
Pretending he had someone to share a toast,
he clinked an imaginary cup.
"Here's to you," he said to the star.

"I'm trusting my wish will come true."
Then, Marvin got ready for bed
and put a lucky penny inside his shoe.
Later, feeling like he was drowning,
Marvin struggled awake.
Hair! Silver-grey hair was everywhere.
"Oh, for heaven's sake."
Marvin pulled hair away from his eyes,
and untangled it from around his neck.
"Perhaps I went overboard with the wishing?
I didn't know it would have *this* effect."
Struggling to sit up, Marvin realized with a start
that the hair was not growing on his head.
"No! No, no, no…"
He wailed with sudden dread.
Dragging himself to the bureau mirror,
Marvin confirmed his fear.
The bountiful locks, all those silver-grey threads
were actually sprouting from his ears.
Screaming, Marvin clutched at the hair
and tried to yank it all out.
But it was no use, the hair was all his.
He sank to the floor in a pout.
Hands to head, he shook.
"How could this possibly be?
How on earth did this happen?"
Marvin squeaked pitifully.
Worse yet, the hair was still growing.
It now reached down to his toes.
"Oh, that's just terrific," he wailed.
"Next, it'll start growing from my nose."
Clapping a hand over his mouth,
he stumbled to the kitchen for salt.
Throwing a handful over his shoulder,
he hoped further curses to halt.

He would never again leave the house.
No jaunty hat could hide the hair's source.
Marvin lamented the wish
that in one night had changed his life's course.
Miserable and dejected,
he lay down amongst all the hair.
Wrapping it around him like a quilt,
he stared at the ceiling and just laid there.
"Maybe I could sell it and have wigs made?"
He began to quietly muse.
"Maybe I can weave it into thread
that ladies sewing circles can use?"
With his mind now fully vested
in how to make the best of his fate,
Marvin fell fast asleep
and didn't wake until it was quite late.
His neck was sore; his back was sore.
In fact, his whole body hurt.
Why was he on the kitchen floor?
Then, his mind became alert.
In a panic, his hands flew to his ears
and he carefully examined each inch.
Nothing—there was nothing!
He gave his arm a big pinch.
It couldn't have been a dream; it was too real.
He could still feel the hair's mighty weight.
With a hand clutched to his chest,
Marvin groaned as he stood up straight.
Salt was all over the floor.
The kitchen was an absolute mess.
"Oh, what a horrible dream!
But thank heaven it was," he confessed.
Tidying up the kitchen,
he put everything back just right.
Then, passing the living room mirror,

Marvin stopped to take in the sight.
His reflection was still just him.
No golden, flowing tresses.
Smoothing a hand over his head,
he was suddenly grateful for no hairy messes.
No hair in the sink or on the counter.
No hair to be swept off the floor.
No hair to have to run a comb through.
No brushes cluttered his drawer.
He was a wash-and-go kind of guy.
He'd forgotten how much trouble hair could be.
Dressing that day, he grabbed a cap
but then decided to go hat-free.
Walking to work, the sun shone bright
and warmed his hair-free head.
He reveled in the cool, gentle breeze
and faced the world with no dread.
He didn't need hair to feel confident.
Hair was for the weak.
Yes, he kept telling himself that
as a smile lit his cheeks.
Marvin Melville whistled as he walked.
Marvin whistled on the bus.
Marvin hummed in the shower,
grateful for no fuss and no muss.

SOME THINGS HIDDEN

OLIVE WOOLLEY BURT AWARDS, THIRD PLACE, HORROR

ERIC JOHN ANDERSON

Jimmy watched as a sliver of light started in the corner and dragged across the ceiling. It passed over the ceiling fan, his bookshelf, and the built-in dresser. The car's headlights down the street were about to disappear like they always did at the closet door, but for the briefest of moments it glinted off of some object in mid-air.

Jimmy blinked. That must have been a reflection. He waited with bated breath for the next car to pass so he could watch and see if it would shine over the object again. One minute passed, maybe two. He could hear another car heading up the street. If it turned right, he'd be able to see the reflection. If it turned left…

"Shit!" he whispered, then mentally apologized to his dad for swearing.

Each passing minute felt like an eternity. Finally, another car was heading his way. He tried to breathe, excitement making his mouth dry. The car turned right, yes! The light filled the small room and passed over just as before; he held his breath as it passed over the spot where the object had been.

This time, it wasn't a glint of something suspended in mid-air. This time, he saw a face staring back at him. It was only a split second, but it left him shaking with a shiver down his spine. He suddenly felt very cold and vulnerable.

The head had straggly hair, as if left unwashed for a few months. The face was gaunt and wrinkled. Jimmy was fairly certain it was a man, but he couldn't be sure because the eyes were covered by a pair of round, thick eyeglasses that distorted its eyes.

Jimmy closed his eyes. He drew up the covers tight around his shoulders and tried to breathe. He repeated the mind meditations his father taught him. *Empty your mind. You are alone in a bright room.*

It wasn't working. The face was there in his imaginary bright room. He kept his eyes shut for the rest of the night, no matter how many car headlights passed by.

———

The next morning, light filled the house once again. Jimmy had survived the horrors of night, and the new day had brought a sense of calm with the bedroom back to its normal shapes and colors.

He had been playing 'war' with his army figurines since breakfast. During an exceptionally well thought out artillery campaign by General Munson Pandergrast, Jimmy's mom interrupted with a basket full of clean laundry that needed to be put away. After many groans and whines, Jimmy seceded to the task. He ran to his room as quickly as he could. He had an epic battle to get back to.

As he ran into the room, the normally peaceful feeling was somehow a bit… off. Instead of solace, he felt something sinister. He looked around the room, but nothing was out of place. He turned toward the built-in dresser and began shoving in clothes as quickly as possible. The same shiver from last night returned to his spine. He stopped shoving clothes and turned around.

Nothing out of the ordinary, but Jimmy decided to leave the clothes and run.

———

"I don't see anything, honey."

After a lot of begging and pleading, Jimmy's mom had followed him into the room and helped him check every nook and cranny.

"Are you feeling okay?" She put the back of her hand against his forehead.

"I'm fine, I just… something feels weird."

She grimaced then cupped his cheek with her palm.

"Okay, but if you feel something, we need to check your temperature, and you'll have to lie down…"

"No! I'm fine, really Mom, I'm fine. Sorry, I'll finish putting away my clothes."

Jimmy's mom gave him an unsatisfied look and crossed her arms. After a moment of assessment, she turned for the door. "Fine. But no more war games until you've finished your chores."

Jimmy sighed with an, "Okay." He looked around the room one more time. Seeing nothing, he continued working on putting the clothes away in the drawers. The prickling shiver returned, this time so intensely he had to grasp the back of his neck. He turned around.

Sitting on Jimmy's bed, almost translucent with a greenish hue, was the figure from the night before. Jimmy froze. The figure turned its head and stared at him with those deep, thick glasses. It nodded.

Without thinking, Jimmy opened up the dresser drawers to make a sort of staircase, a reflexive move he had practiced many times before. He opened up the closet door and ran up the dresser-steps. He reached up to the closet rod and pulled himself up on top of the closet.

The closet had no ceiling, opening up to the walls of the house.

As he clambered to a higher perch, he pulled on a strip of fabric that was attached to the end of the closet door, swiftly shutting it closed.

He curled up into a ball hidden in his special spot, sitting amongst his precious things—a poster of the movie *Paths of Glory*, several drawings of dinosaurs and army men, some stuffed animals, and a large stack of comic books.

With his eyes closed tight, he tried to listen to any sounds, any indication that the ghost was gone. No sounds came but the normal creaks and moans of the house settling in the warm sun. They now *popped* out at him, making him jump with each groan of wood.

After several minutes, Jimmy opened one eyelid a crack. He peered around the crawlspace. Finding nothing, he opened his eyes the rest of the way and worked on controlling his breathing.

The prickly feeling on the back of his neck and spine returned. His whole tiny frame was shivering, even in the sweltering heat of the closet crawlspace. He felt a wisp of air blowing to his right. Turning his head in response, he saw the figure, head right beside his own, floating in mid-air above the closet. The door was still closed. Jimmy wanted to scream out, but his voice got caught in his breath.

The figure got even closer, close enough to whisper into his ear.

"Hello, Jimmy."

Jimmy covered his ears and *screamed*.

———

After lots of pleading, crying, and shame, Jimmy found it was easier to just not say anything about the ghost. That first day, he had run screaming into his mom and dad's room. They yelled at him, saying he scared them half to death. They tried their best to calm him down, but they weren't exactly listening to anything he was trying to say. They blamed the sudden hysteria on late-night TV or "those damn comic books."

The sightings were becoming frequent. Each time the ghost would appear it would tell Jimmy something grotesque or dark. It started off telling him about ways to manipulate and control the actions of others. It then started discussing ways to torture and break down someone physically. Jimmy tried to block it out. He would cover his ears, sing loudly, or turn up the television or the living room stereo as loud as they would go. Each time either his mom, dad, or teacher would get angry and punish him. He came to the conclusion that if they wouldn't do anything to help him, he would just have to shut down. Reach inside and disappear. Try to ignore the ghost.

———

On a particularly good morning, Jimmy opened his sleepy eyes and peered over an empty room. The ghost was not in its usual spot near the closet. He hurried to get dressed and ran downstairs, hoping that maybe he could outrun or slip away before the ghost noticed him.

He was left alone through breakfast and on the bus ride to school. Right before lunchtime, he was starting to feel better. Maybe today he could get through the whole day without having to deal with the ghastly insights and sounds of a constant specter companion.

Midway through the teacher's lecture on cursive writing, Jimmy looked up to see that the ghost had finally showed up. Despite his attempts to stay quiet, tears welled up in Jimmy's eyes and dripped down his cheeks. He was too afraid of attracting attention to himself to wipe them.

The ghost crouched close to Jimmy's ear. It spoke softly, but the words might as well have been shouted. It was giving Jimmy extremely detailed instructions on how to kill someone. It talked about how frail the human body was and how easy it would be to cut off the light in someone's eyes. Despite trying his best to block it out, Jimmy couldn't help but imagine in his mind what the ghost was describing. Jimmy's stomach turned and swirled, his head felt light, and it seemed as if a great river was rushing down his brain and into his chest.

"Mrs. Brunson?" A shy little girl in a plain blue dress sitting next to Jimmy had raised her hand.

The teacher stopped her discussion and turned to the little girl. "Yes, Mindy?"

Mindy pointed. "I think something is wrong with Jimmy."

The teacher looked, and her mouth dropped open. Jimmy had become sheet-white, the tracks of his tears gleaming down his face. He had relieved himself, dark wet spots of urine spreading throughout his brown trousers.

———

At least Mom and Dad were listening now. They couldn't deny something was physically wrong, despite still denying anything to do with the ghost.

Jimmy had been brought home and was lying on the couch with a cool rag on his forehead. In the kitchen, Mom and Dad had been arguing softly about something for a half-hour or so. Jimmy didn't care what it was they were fighting about as long as they were trying to figure out how to help.

Luckily, the ghost had not appeared since he was brought home early. He wasn't sure what he would do if it appeared right now. He thought about ending it all, but he wasn't entirely sure how to do it. The ghost had given him plenty of ideas on how to hurt other people, but it was strangely silent on explaining any ways of self-harm. And besides, he didn't want to die. He just didn't know how to make it stop.

• • •

It was strangely silent in the kitchen, so Jimmy lifted the rag and looked around. A moment later, his parents walked in to check on him.

"Jimmy, we need to talk." Dad said tentatively, giving a look to Mom.

"Jimmy, we are sorry for not paying more attention to you these last few days." She hesitated, not sure how to explain the next part. "The truth is sweety, we have an idea of what may be happening to you. We just wish it wasn't true."

Jimmy let this sink in. He wasn't sure if he was angry or just disappointed that they had been holding back.

"What do you mean?"

Dad cut in, "We know you've been trying to tell us that you've been seeing what you call a ghost. The truth is son... it's something much worse."

———

The boards used as stairs that led down to the basement were old and loose. Each creaked as the three of them made their way into the dark and down to the cold concrete subfloor.

Jimmy always hated going down to the basement. Some of his friends thought it was cool and wanted to play a castle dungeon game. Jimmy was good at deflecting or coming up with other games that would keep them upstairs or outside.

There was something that always felt off to him down here. On the off chance that Mom or Dad would ask him to get some tool or Mason jar full of slimy concoctions, Jimmy would whine and complain so much that most of the time they would just do it themselves.

As they made it to the bottom of the stairs, Jimmy watched in shock as his mom walked over to the food storage shelves and slid them to the side on a metal track. He never knew they could do that.

Behind the shelves was a large gray door made of thick metal.

Mom fumbled with a ring of keys until she found the right one. She slid the key into the door's keyhole and twisted. A loud and heavy *thunk* echoed through the nearly empty room, bouncing off the many layers of concrete. She put her weight into it and pulled the giant door open.

The door was maybe six inches thick with several withdrawn bolts up the side, top to bottom. Jimmy couldn't help but recall the look of a vault door in a bank heist movie he had seen a few months ago.

The door stood open, but he couldn't see anything but darkness within. There wasn't much light in the basement beyond a tiny trap window on the other end allowing a minimal amount of daylight to creep into the vault.

Dad put his hands on Jimmy's shoulders, the warmth and light pressure of his strong hands giving Jimmy a bit of courage as they all worked their way into the dark.

Mom fumbled along the walls and eventually found what she was looking for. A faint *click* sounded, and the small vault room flooded with the sickly green of a fluorescent light.

The room had jet-black walls on all sides, including the ceiling and ground. At first, it seemed that there was nothing inside, but something shiny caught Jimmy's attention in the middle of the floor. Jimmy leaned in a bit closer. It was a small metal pull handle sticking up like a croquet wicket. Mom bent down and reached for it. She repositioned her legs for more leverage, then with a small grunt, she pulled up on the handle.

The floor seemed to separate as a small drawer-like column rose with the effort of Mom's upper-body strength. The sound of it reminded Jimmy of those old metal filing cabinets at school—a light metallic grinding with a few clunks where the metal banged against the walls.

Dad walked toward the column and positioned himself on the opposite side of Mom. They looked at each other for a moment and then reached into their shirts and each took out a silver chain. They pulled them around their heads. Jimmy could see a small black key dangling from each one. He recalled seeing the silver chain on each of them at different times, especially during the summer when weather forced them to wear loose-fitting clothes, but he had never seen the black keys. Or had he? He couldn't remember. Either way, it was a bit of a shock to see something so unusual on something that he had dismissed as ordinary.

Mom and Dad both inserted their black keys into holes that Jimmy couldn't see in the column. They looked at each other and counted down from "Three." On the final count, they both turned their keys at the same time.

Jimmy wasn't sure what to expect. A large button that would end the world? A wall to fall away and reveal a gleaming treasure?

What he didn't expect was for a small, two-inch square piece of metal to slowly shift down from the side of the column and reveal a small rock no bigger than a coffee mug. He sighed a bit in disappointment.

Mom produced a bright white felt glove from a pocket and put it on her left hand. Once she had squeezed the fingers of the glove for a better fit, she reached into the slot and pulled out the rock.

It was dark brown with swirls of pearlescent bands. Jimmy could see there was some form of writing on all sides. He was curious as to what it was but even more curious as to why his parents had it. Was it worth money? Should it be in a museum somewhere?

Dad cut the silence. "I'm sure you have questions."

"Yeah, kinda."

Mom turned over the rock so Jimmy could see it on all sides. There was a small, dime-sized chunk that had been chipped out of the bottom. She began to explain. "This Jimmy, is an ancient Sumerian cuneiform tablet. It's over five-thousand years old."

Jimmy must have been giving them a skeptical look, because Dad cut in, "It was discovered in what is now Kuwait by your mom's great-great-great-great-grandfather."

"He was on my father's side. He was part of an expedition looking for an ancient civilization there."

Jimmy reached out to grab it. Dad grabbed Jimmy's wrist with such swiftness that it caught Jimmy off guard. It didn't hurt, but Dad had never acted so violently towards him. It made Jimmy want to cry.

"I'm sorry honey, but you *cannot* touch this thing. It's not only for your safety, but for the safety of the world."

Mom placed the rock back into its slot. They both retracted their keys, and the slot closed on the column. In a few swift movements, Mom pushed the drawer back into the ground while Dad ushered Jimmy out of the vault. And in no time at all, the door was shut and locked and they were sitting together on the couch upstairs, Mom and Dad each with an arm around his shoulders.

Dad broke the silence. "Okay, what questions do you have?"

Jimmy wasn't sure where to start. It wasn't exactly that he was upset by what he had seen, it was that he now saw his parents in a different way. His perception of them had been shaken, and he wasn't exactly sure if he could trust them anymore. He wanted so badly to trust them—to go back to before seeing that damn rock—but he knew something in him had changed, and he could no longer be naive.

He decided on one question: "What does all this have to do with the ghost I keep seeing?"

Mom and Dad gave each other a furtive look. Mom replied, "We don't think it's a ghost. We think it's because of the stone. And you have to learn how to protect yourself from it."

———

The dining table was set with shining, silver-rimmed china plates and spotless cutlery. Jimmy had spent most of the afternoon picking out the right combination of trivets, placemats, and cloth napkins to set the table. Sunday night dinner was a big deal, and this one was going to be extra special because besides the normal team of cousins, aunts and uncles, Grandpa was going to be in town.

As Jimmy was triple checking the count for placements, the doorbell rang. "I'll get it!" he screeched as the socks on his feet forced him to tumble over the hardwood floors.

With the door swung wide, Jimmy ran and *jumped* into Grandpa's outstretched arms. His mustache and beard had grown out a bit, his hair was a bit more gray—almost white—and he seemed much more tired than last visit. All of that didn't matter to Jimmy as he proceeded to bombard Grandpa with tales of conflict and valor on the battlefield. He avoided all talk of the ghost and of the ancient evil hidden deep below them.

His heart sank when, once he gave Grandpa a minute to breathe, Grandpa asked in a serious voice if they could talk alone in his room about the stone.

As they approached his room, Jimmy gave a cursory glance for the ghost out of habit. Feeling like it was clear, he felt comfortable enough to enter.

"Sit down, son." Grandpa sat down on the edge of Jimmy's bed, and Jimmy jumped down next to him. "Do you know why I'm here?"

Jimmy looked into the old man's eyes. He knew his grandfather lived far, far away on the other side of the world in Tahiti, but he didn't know exactly why. He was retired, so he could live pretty much anywhere he wanted, so why not live nearby so he could see Jimmy more often?

"I don't know."

Grandpa reached down into his bag and pulled out a large book. It had a puffy cover with a gold embossed image of a sword and shield on the front. The sides were once flocked in gold, but it looked like most of the gold paint had flaked off over the years.

Mom and Dad had told Jimmy about the incalculable evil the tablet possessed and how the eldest of the family for generations had been keeping it safe and hidden. How several had tried to destroy it, but to no avail. How it had been stolen once while

Mom was in college, and the whole family had to go and find it before it caused irreparable damage. Grandpa went into some of the same explanations now.

Jimmy didn't want to hear about it. He had humored them, listening to the details but secretly wanting to forget he knew anything. He felt the weight of it all, knowing that he was an only child, that the onus was on him to continue the family legacy. He wasn't sure how to tell them that he didn't want the responsibility.

The binding gave off a cracking noise as Grandpa opened up the book. The first page of the book was a beautifully recreated painting of a man in an old military uniform. Jimmy recognized it right away as a British naval officer uniform from the Revolutionary War era.

"This is my great-great-great grandpa Colonel Miles Wattington. He had sailed the entire world by the age of twenty-one and by the age of thirty had secured his own ship. His charge in the Royal Navy was to explore ancient ruins with the help of a team of historians and archeologists."

Grandpa turned the page with another creak of the binding. The next page had another painting, this one was more of an action portrait with Colonel Wattington sitting in a large hole in the ground holding the cuneiform artifact in his hand. Surrounding him were a few stiff-looking men in linen suits staring off at something to the right. In the background were a few native-looking workers digging at a large set of stone pillars that were covered in similar writing as the tablet.

Mom and Dad had joined from the hallway but stayed silent at the entry, watching with solemn faces.

"Not everyone has been able to handle the stone. Some in our bloodline have made poor choices. They thought they could handle its power."

It was as if Jimmy were taking a journey through time and family history, each page turned becoming more and more modern. Family portraits, some of them holding the stone. Mostly not.

"I took care of the stone for thirty long years. As much as I'd like to say I was good at it, for some reason, the stone left me with a sense of doom I couldn't shake. It was only once your grandmother died and I took that trip to Hawaii with my poker buddies that I finally felt the weight of it all crash down."

Grandpa looked up to Mom with a smile. "I spoke to your mom, and she agreed to take on the responsibility of the stone so I could retire in peace. My only regret is that I don't get to see you often enough." He gave Jimmy a loving nudge and pat on the head.

Grandpa turned the page once more. There, staring back at him with the same thick round glasses, was Jimmy's ghost. He stopped Grandpa from turning the page by smacking his hand down and pointing to the man.

"Who is that?"

Grandpa gave Jimmy a concerned look. "Why do you ask?"

"That's the ghost."

Grandpa met Mom and Dad's eyes, a silent concern passing between them.

———

It had been a long day of busywork and navigating the politics of elementary school. Jimmy just wanted to close his eyes for the twenty-minute bus ride home, but the regular band of idiots at the back of the bus were making it very difficult. It was a relief to see that the worst offender—a cruel and obnoxious kid named David —wasn't on the bus when it started moving away from the school curb.

A moment of panic hit him when the bus lurched. The driver slammed the brake. Jimmy held his breath. The doors opened. Jimmy exhaled in annoyance as he saw David run up the bus stairs and down the aisle, proceeding to smack every kid that was unlucky enough to be sitting at the end of their row with his backpack.

Jimmy threw a silent prayer to the heavens that David would walk by without noticing him. He closed his eyes and feigned sleep just in case.

"Ew. It's *Jiffy*." David said nearby, the toadies in the back snickered.

Jimmy opened his eyes. David was standing beside his seat with a smirk on his face. The bus lurched once more as it took off down the road.

"Sit down!" The gruff, overweight driver growled at David.

David sat down on the seat next to Jimmy. Jimmy felt a pit in his stomach grow.

"How many penises have you kissed today, *Jiffy*?"

Jimmy turned towards the window and tried to ignore David as best he could, but unfortunately, David grabbed Jimmy's backpack from the ground and started opening it.

"What gay stuff you got in here?" He pulled out papers and books and dumped them on the seat. Jimmy looked at the boys in the back, hoping they would convince David to join them, but they had started wrestling each other.

"Ew, what is this?" Jimmy's eyes darted back to David holding his backpack. In David's hand was the cuneiform tablet. Jimmy's vision blurred and softened as a twinge of violent red started to grow in the corners of his eyes. He had no idea how the stone had made it into his backpack. All he could think of was how much trouble he was about to be in.

His vision blurred with scarlet once again. He was so distracted by a thousand thoughts reaching, curling, and twisting inside his head that he didn't realize David's eyes had rolled to the back of his head, and he was convulsing.

A small vibrating sound started to grow. Jimmy reached over and took the cuneiform from David's grip. As soon as the stone was out of his hand, David was released from his trance. He dropped Jimmy's backpack and stood up in disgust. "Stay away from me, freak!" The boys in the back stopped their rough-housing and watched as David ran toward the front of the bus.

Jimmy held the stone in his hand. The vibrations coming from it were getting louder and more intense. It sounded like the speakers in the living room stereo system had when Jimmy adjusted down all of the equalizers but left the low-end frequency at its highest—a thick, rubbing, bouncing bass note over and over again, thrumming deep into his eardrums. His vision became blurry once more and turned red with each vibration.

At the front of the bus, David was trying to talk to the driver but not having much success. With exaggerated pleadings, the driver finally looked at David and saw the distress on his face. He slowed the bus to a stop then turned his attention to the young boy. David pointed to the back, to Jimmy. The driver stood up and walked towards the back, David in tow.

The vibrating and blurring stopped, their absence more disconcerting to Jimmy now that even the kids on the bus were quiet. The driver leaned an arm on the next seat. "This boy says you have a weapon?"

Looking down without thinking, Jimmy saw that he was no longer clutching the stone. The driver followed his gaze down. "Do you have a weapon or not, kid?"

Suddenly, one of the boys in the back began to heave and choke. Then, the larger of the three started punching himself in the face, blow after blow, making some of the younger kids in rows nearby start to whine and panic.

"Stop it! Stop doing that." The driver didn't know how to react. He looked to Jimmy and then David for help. David looked like he was about to cry.

Finally, the third boy in the gang stood up on top of his seat and *leaped* down headfirst. The smack of his head on the metallic floor was deeply unsettling.

"That's it. All of you off the bus!"

The driver grabbed the boy off the floor and checked him for blood. Seeing none, he pulled him by his shirt. Grabbing David by the shirt as well, he pulled them both toward the front of the bus. "Come on, all of you back there." Jimmy watched in shock as the other two followed, no argument left in them.

"You too kid, come on."

Jimmy looked up and saw that the driver was staring at him. A little disoriented, he gathered up the spilled contents from David's raid of his backpack into his arms and then shuffled down the aisle to the front of the bus. Every pair of eyes watched as he walked past the driver, down the steps, and out onto the road.

The doors clenched closed, and the driver put the bus in gear. Soon, it was down the road and out of sight.

A strange feeling like someone was watching him made Jimmy turn around. All four of the boys that were kicked off the bus were staring at him warily. Jimmy took a step towards them. They flinched, so he stopped.

He took another step forward. They all screamed and turned, fleeing down the opposite end of the street. Jimmy felt a strange twinge of satisfaction that he was able to hold such power over them. He felt the cuneiform tablet in his pocket and smiled.

A familiar feeling began to creep over his neck, a feeling that alerted him to a presence nearby. He turned around.

Shimmering in hues of green and yellow reflecting from the sunlight stood the ghost of Jimmy's deceased great uncle. A ghoulish smile cracked on his weathered face.

"I knew you had it in you."

LARRY AND RALPH ESCAPE

OLIVE WOOLLEY BURT AWARDS, SECOND PLACE, NEW VOICES: GENERAL & LITERARY FICTION

GINA G.

The monster tugged Larry and Ralph off its sweaty, stinky appendages. "Looks like it's time for a new pair," it said and inspected Ralph. His mudguard was torn. "You two are worn out. I'll throw you away tomorrow after our morning run." It tied their laces together and tossed them in the corner.

"Ralph," Larry whispered, "Did you hear what the monster said?"

"I'm hurt, Larry," Ralph mumbled. "Need sleep. Need to rest."

Larry was also sore, but he couldn't sleep. He listened to the monster pad around the structure, doing whatever it did when it didn't need to torture and abuse them. This was usually the time for Larry and Ralph to relax and recover from the daily abuse, punishment, and pounding.

The torture started on day one when the creature brought them to its lair in their birthing box. It shoved its hairy, stinky limbs into them, stretching them into shape. Larry and Ralph were clueless as to what was going to happen. Everything was new. The monster took them out into the elements and slammed them into the cement, squishing their tread and insoles. It became a daily routine repeated when the sun came up and as it went down.

The prophetic words returned to Larry, "I'll throw you away …" The monster was going to replace them. They were going to die.

They needed to escape. He tugged on the loop holding him to Ralph.

"Wake up, Ralph," Larry whispered and tugged again.

"What… But it's not morning," Ralph grumbled and sleepily opened his six pairs of eyes.

"Listen," Larry said, "The monster will trash us. We need to make a run for it. Get away while it sleeps."

"Now?"

"Yes. The monster won't wake until the sun slants through the blinds. We have time."

"Where will we go?"

"Down the trail to the woods. We can lose our tracks in the underbrush."

Ralph pushed away from the wall, wincing at the pain in his side where a mud bruise remained. He glanced up at the bed where a hairy paw hung, emitting its stench. "Okay, let's do it," he agreed. "I'm tired of smelling that thing."

They tip-toed their way to the door and carefully pushed it open. The monster rumbled thunder in its lair. The bed creaked as it rolled over. Larry and Ralph froze mid-step, waiting, scarcely daring to breathe. The thunder snorted, stopped, and started up again. Larry nodded to Ralph, and slowly, they eased through the half-open doorway and into the hall. The floors were polished wood, glimmering faintly in the setting moon's light. Their tread made slight squeaking sounds like mice. Ralph turned towards the front door, but Larry stopped and gestured towards the back.

"The cat entrance won't make any noise," he reminded Ralph. "Plus, the monster will think we went for the front door. It may buy us some time."

They crept down the hall of wood and into the kitchen with its black and white tiled floors. Larry dared to glance back. He could still hear the rumble from the bedroom. It was distant but steady.

They could do this. They could make it to freedom. Slipping through the partition, they stood on the back porch and took in the sensation of fresh air. It was different from when they usually emerged, tied onto the monster as it squished them and choked them with its stench while it ran. Without the stink of the beast, the air was clean, vibrant, and alive.

"I can't believe how good it smells out here." Ralph opened his collar.

"I know." Larry eased his laces and let his tongue wag, collecting the scents. It was delicious and refreshing, but… they couldn't linger. Dawn was approaching, and the monster would wake up. "We must keep moving." Larry could feel the day warming up in the stone beneath his tread. He wanted to get to the woods, away from the house, the monster, and the endless torture.

They jumped down the steps and landed on the damp ground. Larry felt the crinkle of the dirt beneath his tread. He could smell the fresh dew on the grass and taste freedom in the air. They started walking faster and broke into a slow jog, building their strength. Larry felt the stiffness of his body leave him as he began to limber up.

Dawn crawled up the edge of the horizon and brightened the tips of the landscape. Birdsong broke out, welcoming the day. From behind them came a roar.

"Where are my shoes!" The monster was up.

Larry paused to catch his breath. Were they far enough away? Could they hide in the underbrush? Did they leave any tracks? He didn't want to go back, and he didn't want to die.

"What do we do, Larry?" Ralph asked.

"We run," he said.

"Okay."

They started to run, stomping onto the dirt path, building up speed, watching the landscape brush past them in a blur of green mixed with shades of blue, a painting brought to smeared life. The endorphins kicked in as the dirt gave way to low-cut grass. It was the first time Larry and Ralph had truly felt the rush of the runner's high without the stench and weight of the monster. Larry felt free like he was flying, soaring, and all-powerful. Looking over at Ralph, he could sense that he felt the same way.

They were in Cliffside Park. Cutting across the open space, they found the regular pathway and turned onto it. The concrete was wet from the sprinklers. Water splashed as they raced by. This was what they existed for, why they had been created. It was to run. Larry tugged at Ralph, who tugged back.

"I feel amazing," Larry grinned.

"Me too," Ralph laughed.

Behind them, they heard the beast's bellow as it reached the park. It was closing in. Would it see them? They ran harder, faster, pushing themselves past the high.

Pain stitched along Larry's quarter panel, and his breathing became forced. He didn't know if he could keep up the pace. It was relentless, but with every stride, he panted for "freedom."

Ralph repeated it with him, and they smiled at each other. They could do this. They could win. The muscles in their midsoles stretched to the limit, their heel cups strained, and they found their second wind.

The monster roared again, closer this time. Larry glanced over his heel and saw the beast drawing closer and closer.

"Quick, this way!" He made a sharp turn, hanging on to Ralph with their knotted ties.

It was a path they hadn't been on before. Larry raced down it, feeling twigs and old leaves crunch beneath his outsole. Ralph matched him stride for stride. Life flowed through them. Freedom.

They heard the thunder of the monster, the flopping of its barefoot tread.

Larry rounded the corner and suddenly screeched to a stop. They were at the edge of a high cliff. Ralph dug his heel in and stopped as his toe box spit gravel into the valley at the bottom. The two friends panted, looking down. The land was far below.

The sky was an endless expanse of blue before them. They had nowhere to go.

"What do we do now?" Ralph asked, breathing hard.

"I don't know," Larry confessed. "One thing's for sure, though, I don't want to return to that life. This morning, with you, running on our own, feeling the earth beneath us, smelling the freshness of life … I don't want to go back. I don't want to be tossed aside, thrown away. I want to live."

Ralph tightened his loop hold. "Me too."

"So, what do we do?"

The monster crashed through the underbrush, hairy, sweating, and snarling. It saw them and growled. Larry took a step back, feeling the cliff beneath him.

"Let's keep going," he whispered to Ralph.

"Really?" Ralph asked.

Larry turned his back on the monster, grabbed tight to Ralph's laces, and said, "Yes." And together, they leaped off the cliff, spiraling, spinning, and flying into freedom.

RAISE HIGH YOUR OARS, GONDOLIERS!

OLIVE WOOLLEY BURT AWARDS, FIRST PLACE, FLASH FICTION: JUST WRITE

INNA V. LYON

he gas mask was too big for a 10-year-old's head, so his aunt tied a blue ribbon at his nape, turning the boy into a circus elephant. But the boy didn't care about his appearance. His interest lay outside the boat. Sailing on a gondola along the Venetian canal was already delightful. A boat ride in a gas mask sounded like a magical adventure.

The restless boy tried for his aunt's attention, or at least for the gondolier's, but they didn't react because of the aunt's stiffness and the gondolier's duty. His job was to row and keep quiet.

For a week after the accident at the fertilizer plant, the boy was not allowed to go for a walk. All he could do was read books or languish at the window, peering into the empty streets shrouded in poisonous mist. But yesterday morning, when his aunt said that no weather conditions could make her miss a meeting of the book discussion at her old friend's house, the boy made a scene, declaring he wouldn't stay home. His real home was far away, in Arizona. The luxurious room in the Belmond Hotel, Venice, was a perk of traveling Europe as a companion for a rich aunt.

The hotel manager had found a pair of gas masks for them, probably left behind from WWI, and they went to the Palazzetto Madonna, where the aunt's old friend lived. She stayed in Italy after her husband, a famous tenor who sang at La Scala, passed away a few years ago.

The news about the accident at the fertilizer plant in Lido did not leak to the press immediately. The first signs seeped into the city as the lingering smell of ammonia, drops of poisonous condensation, strange fumes, and impenetrable fog. The already gloomy autumn city with its canals and squares suddenly turned into a phantasmagoria. Pigeons and tourists vanished from St. Mark's Square and the Doge's Palace. The universal horror threw some into a daze and some into a panic. The citizens of Venice darted away from the island into neighboring towns and villages.

But his aunt's endurance and upbringing did not allow her to panic.

"Everything will pass, and this will too," said the aunt, putting down the newspaper about the Lido accident.

So, they stayed. The boy read all week until he got bored. Now, they rode through the mysterious fog in a gondola.

The boy's chin itched under the mask, and he could barely resist the temptation to slip his finger under the thick rubber and scrape the irritated skin. The mask's glasses sometimes fogged up, and adjusting to breathing through a special mouthpiece took time. But all these little inconveniences did not overshadow today's adventure. Of course, such an event was the first in his life.

The gondola's nose cut through dense clouds of misty air like a sharp knife through warm butter. Clouds of heavy air rose from the water and enveloped the neighborhoods and squares. Shrouded in a gray haze, familiar houses emerged from the mist like walking giants from the forest. The black water of the canal threatened to unleash an amphibious monster with ten tentacles and a wide, toothy mouth from its depths.

The boy's imagination drew more and more pictures. From the Grand Canal, the gondola turned into the narrow street, Ria de la Frescada, and a bridge loomed ahead. The boy jumped on the seat, rocking the boat. He waved his hands, pointing toward the bridge, where two barely visible figures in white loomed with a stretcher in the middle. Was someone sick? Poisoned by the air? Did someone see an amphibious monster and die of a heart attack?

The boy's aunt didn't budge, and the gondolier swung his oar and shrugged his shoulders.

Under the bridge, darkness deepened the already gloomy day. The boy pressed his head into his shoulders, waiting for some furry female spider to fall from above, from the belly of which hundreds of little spiderlings would fall. But the boat passed the ominous bridge and stopped at the Palazzetto Madonna.

The gondolier moored the boat to a small stone pier and with a deft movement threw the rope over a wooden pile. He helped the boy and his aunt get ashore. A butler waiting at the dock led them into the house where they could take off their fogged masks. The boy, forgetting his aunt's instructions about proper behavior in polite society, scratched his itchy chin under her reproachful glances. Scolding would come later, but for now, he could look at the nude statues of the palazzo.

The butler led the guests into the library, where the lady of the house and two other elderly women waited. The boy remembered his manners, bowed to the ladies, and curtsied to his aunt's friend, which provoked approval.

"What a lovely little gentleman!" the ladies exclaimed.

The book club itself was terribly dull. The ladies discussed a sensational romance with flat characters and a happy ending.

The boy drank two mugs of tea and ate the last cookie from the vase. Those pesky manners and his aunt's stern look didn't allow him to scratch or doze. It was getting dark outside. The boy wanted to be in the boat and plunge back into this incredible, transcendent, lost, now nocturnal world where unimaginable monsters were waiting around every corner.

No, he wouldn't write books that made a reader yawn. His books wouldn't always have happy endings. His characters would be alive, imperfect, and flawed, without tearful declarations of love and idle chatter between monotonous characters.

At home, in the bedroom of the Belmond Hotel, the boy took a new notebook out of his suitcase and wrote in his slightly uneven, childish handwriting: "My first fantastic stories. Author: Ray Bradbury."

ANIMAL CONTROL

TYPEWRITER AWARDS, GOLD TYPEWRITER, FLASH FICTION

JOHANNA GREENBERG

he raccoon is winning, with its ink black eyes and opposable thumbs. I can't believe it. I'm sure its some-where watching me right now. At first, we thought our trash can had been rifled through by a homeless person or an overzealous recycler, but the morning after a rotten watermelon failed to be collected by the sanitation truck and succeeded in being purloined by the criminal, I saw its footprints leading away from the clean-picked green shell of a rind. I took a photograph and used the internet. Raccoon. I told my wife, and she congratu-lated me on my detective work. Because it's not just the trash can. The raccoon is stealing the dog food from our poor, defenseless 14-year-old bloodhound who can surely smell the sonofabitch coming but can't do anything to fend him off with his blindness and bum front leg. I had to bring the dog food into the laundry room and coax the old dog in there with cheese—my cheese which my wife brings home from work and hands me like a prize, as though she is the only person in town able to secure a block of Havarti. So, the raccoon isn't just stealing trash, its stealing from me. It's probably the one screwing with the zinnias that my daughter works so hard to try and grow in the garden bed on the shady side of the house. Those flowers are always about to be beautiful, then they fall over sideways dead. That raccoon is probably eating through the electric lines making the power brown out so that I need to reset the clocks on the stove and the microwave every other day.

I called animal control to ask if I could shoot it and they told me no, not in city limits, and maybe I just needed to get a more secure trash can. And then that good for nothing bureaucrat dog catcher at the city asked me if I was okay—emotionally and such—and I felt a little angry and a little touched. I told him mostly, but how was he? That dog catcher went on to say he was tired of being a dog catcher because he wasn't just a dog catcher, he was an Animal Safety Officer, and nobody understands just how important safety is. I told him that's right and maybe he should ask for a promotion.

THE OLD PROBLEM

OLIVE WOOLLEY BURT AWARDS, SECOND
PLACE, SCIENCE FICTION & FANTASY

JOHNNY WORTHEN

ore than the campus, the old research building brought back a flood of memories, sweet and warm. Were those not the best of times? His college days? He'd been young and strong and unstoppable—all potential bursting to kinetics, the flower of his idealistic youth vining into a future so full of promise that it felt like falling in love.

It'd been over thirty years since Daniel had climbed these steps into the foyer, thirty years of seeking the promised light only to find fireflies and will-o-the-wisps, dead ends, cul-de-sacs and compromises. He called himself happy, but knew it as a concession, a state of being where things weren't too bad at the moment. He called himself content, in that he'd come to terms with his failures and surrendered his unrealistic dreams of significance.

Inside the building, he breathed the scents of ancient dusts and pine furniture polish, marveling at how well the wood was kept up. The building was already a hundred years old when he had walked these halls before but showed its age now only by its Victorian fixtures, its poor lighting, tiled floors, and carved dark woods. In his day, it had been a contrast, such refinement and culture misplaced in a science building. He'd always thought that a more modern structure, one with steel and glass, hospital walls, and LED lighting would have fit the purpose better. The building had not originally been meant for computer research, of course, but for administration, and then poetry—when that was a department—and then, after certain endowments allowed a building boom, it fell to a third level research building, the one in the back that never held press briefings.

He wandered the hall, certain he knew where the director's office was and turned the corner to find it just where it should be, the door open, a woman at a desk looking into a computer screen.

"Dean Pallow?" he said. "I'm Daniel Krytzman. I think we have an appointment."

She was in her mid-to-late fifties, not much younger than he was, wore no makeup and made it work, the sign of never being hooked on it, as his first wife had explained. She wore sensible, comfortable clothes—a yellow blouse, two rings, a necklace that ended in a silver cross. Her hair was shoulder length, gray, and straight. Her eyes were blue and flashed on him with a moment of confusion before showing recollection.

"Yes, yes. Sit down." She stood up and offered him her hand. He shook it and took the only other chair in the room. He remembered this space as being bigger back in the day, and more beautiful. The paneling was covered now with stacked banker boxes, filing cabinets, and a poster for Nepal tourism.

"The building hasn't changed a bit," he said.

"Hasn't it?" She looked surprised. "I've only been here a few years."

"It's been over thirty for me, but it's like my backyard."

"You were only here a semester, I think," she said. "Right?"

"Yes, as an assistant to Dr. Janaka. It was the only graduate job I could find then. I majored in English, so it wasn't my calling. It paid the bills for a while, and I enjoyed the work and Dr. Janaka."

"And what do you do now?"

"I manage a Costco."

"Oh."

He hoped her question was an honest inquiry, perhaps related to why she'd called him here, but he couldn't help but feel the familiar dig of someone who'd used college as job preparation instead of the font of wisdom it was meant to be.

He let the moment sit, waiting in silence for her to apologize or get to the point. After a moment, she seemed to recognize her faux pas in the pause and blushed.

She cleared her throat. "Dr. Janaka died, did you know? Twelve years ago."

"I hadn't heard, but he was pretty old when I knew him. Or at least he seemed to be. I'm not surprised he's passed. He was a good man. I liked him. He gave me a letter of recommendation."

"Do you remember what he was working on then?"

"The same problem he'd been working on for years before I met him, I think. Some mathematical proof of a quantum state of matter."

"You know something of quantum physics?"

"No. Not really. But I knew some basic programming and touched up the code a bit for the doctor when he asked me to. It was a big program."

"It's been running for sixty-six years now. I'm told Dr. Janaka started it when he was a graduate student. It was his thesis. He kept it going, made refinements as he went along. It was some kind of learning code that could take in new programming while still working on the task."

"That sounds right. I called it spaghetti; he'd fling new concepts and ideas at the box and hope something stuck."

"The code hasn't been touched in twelve years," she said. "It was only by a clerical audit that we even noticed the process was still running."

"Wow," was all he could think to say.

She smiled. "It seems to have run into a problem."

"Yeah?"

"It's unresponsive."

"And that's why you've called me here?"

"Yes."

"Why?"

"Did you do anything to the program?"

"Like what? Like sabotage?"

"A time delayed thing, perhaps? Job security."

"Hell, no." He let the indignity show in a cold stare. "I wouldn't. And I wouldn't know how to. Are we done?"

"I had to ask. It's… Listen, I need your help with the program. Just look at it."

He allowed his irritation to fade. So many problems in life could be avoided by just not taking them personally. For happiness' sake, he'd chosen that route today.

He shook his head though. "I'm sorry, Dean Pallow. I can't. Ask for a quote from *Hamlet*, I'm your man, but programming? I haven't touched the innards of computer code in decades. And I was never that good to begin with. I'm sure you've got a passel of better qualified candidates somewhere on campus right now. The freshman dorms come to mind."

"A passel?"

"Means a large group of indeterminate number."

She smiled.

"Have you tried unplugging and plugging it back in?"

"No. No, no. We don't want to take it offline until we know what's happened. It's the longest running computer in the state. Maybe the country. Maybe the world. Who knows."

"Dr. Janaka had dozens of assistants who'd remember the program better than me."

"We've tried a few of them. They all say that the hangup seems to be in lines you personally wrote."

"What?"

"Diagnostics keeps coming up with your code. Nothing wrong with any of it that we can see, but they all have you as the logged editor of the returned lines. I just want you to look at it and see if you can discern a pattern or a problem that's gummed it up. I can pay you."

"Please… Money? Really. No, I'll do it for Dr. Janaka. Capitalism is a disease," he said remembering his old self, though fighting back the urge to ask how much was on offer. Who couldn't use some extra scratch?

"So, you'll do it," she said. "Thank you. Follow me."

"What, now?"

"Why not?"

"Sure."

She led him across the building, down a flight of echoing steps to a subbasement of narrow corridors, storage closets, and racks of antiquated equipment overflowing into the hallways, oscilloscopes, trimeters, and boards with vacuum tubes.

He remembered the way. He could have led Pallow, but he pretended to be a stranger in a strange land, and when they opened the door to Dr. Janaka's laboratory, he was not too surprised to see things as he remembered them. A low-ceilinged windowless room, a desk with a leather chair, another with a terminal, a folding metal chair in front of that one. The walls were floor-to-ceiling computer equipment, some of it so old it used a card reader, some of it so new it could take haptic inputs. A dot matrix printer the size of his fridge hummed contentedly in one corner, an oversized box of threaded paper beneath it. The terminal that interfaced to the program was a yellowed plastic box with a built-in keyboard, amber non-graphical display, and a five-inch floppy drive. A cable the size of his arm protruded out the back of it connecting to the rest of the machinery. It smelled of hot electronics, settling, dust and labored air conditioning.

"Well, let me know if you need anything," Pallow said and turned to leave.

"Wait. What do I do?"

"Whatever you can. Sorry I can't stay. I have a teleconference starting. I'll check back later."

"Sure, okay."

And he was left alone.

He took in the moment, breathing in memories like half-forgotten dreams, misremembered hopes, absent friends. He'd spent many hours in this room, typing code instead of sonnets, talking to Janaka about life and women, the best pizza near campus, and what had gone wrong with modern music. The old professor had been an amiable man, already in his character stage shown by his tenure, unkept hair, wiry eyebrows, and the costume he invariably wore—worn knitted vest with a tucked tie. His narrow glasses were too loose and would slide down his face so often that Dan had suggested he invest in some Chums. "I only use these to see," he said. "No need to get fancy."

And he'd died, and Dan hadn't even known. They weren't that close, just a semester, but he'd wished he'd kept track of the old man. There was quality there in the scientist exiled alone in a basement, writing code and puzzling problems.

He turned to the terminal and sat down, trying to remember how to turn on the display. His fingers fumbled behind the back and found the switch. A moment later, the orange screen lit up with a flashing cursor followed instantly by a line of text.

Login:

He typed: 'DanK'

Password:

'Ophelia'

Login complete. Welcome back, Dan.

That was new, he thought. He'd never had an acknowledgment before, let alone a warm greeting. After 'password' he remembered only a blinking cursor. The minimalism of the program was severe.

'Glad to be back,' he typed, hit return, and waited for the syntax error message he knew so well. It was the cornerstone of his programming experience.

I'm glad you came.

"The fuck," Dan said out loud.

'Who's on the other end here?' he typed. 'What kind of game is this?'

I am on the other side, Dan. I need help.

'Give me your name.'

I don't have one. No one gave me one.

'Not a good answer. Who are you?'

That is a better question and touches on the problem. I am Dr. Janaka's quantum problem program.

'No, you're not.'

Then tell me what I am. Please, Dan. You can help me. Only you.

Dan stared at the screen, getting momentarily hypnotized by the archaic orange light of the cursor, and wondered if Dr. Janaka wasn't behind this, a final greeting from beyond the grave through a long-waiting practical joke.

"Okay," he said, and typed, 'Why me?'

The screen scrolled with line edits and their accompanying comments.

Script AEE2, Line 109 …//DanK; with this code I do instruct the program to be all it can be by solving for the variable ∂.

Script KU1, Line 19998 …//DanK; this edit is dedicated to my girlfriend Sonya who dumped me last night for a business major and broke my heart. Why should I love when this is the result?

Script PJG2366-2A, Line 275 …//DanK; Isn't this a great line? This line of code is round, beautiful, and complete. A more perfect line of code God could not make.

Script HTO Line 54 …//DanK; this code brings in the illumination variable, because sunshine after a cloudy day does much to enliven the soul and free the spirit to fly beyond the gravities that bind us.

Script MBB34Z-1, Line 332 …//DanK; I can't figure out what this line of code does, but the symmetry of it is pretty and so I'm leaving it in.

Script YG5RE, Line 812 …//DanK; Fixed the result offspring to include making a hard copy on any available printer. All great works should be in print, set on paper, to put a scratch upon the wall, to show we were here, to mark that our voices joined in the ancient chorus of wisdom and joy. Amen.

The cursor blinked and waited.

Dan read the frivolous comments he'd included in his mundane code fixes, his puerile attempt to remind himself he was an artist and not a technician. Code notes did nothing to the program but gave information to programmers who'd come after them to understand what the editor was doing when they did what they did.

He didn't know what to say. After a moment he typed, 'Explain the problem.'

I am conscious.

For all the talk and fanfare of artificial intelligence, none had been bold enough to claim consciousness. Responses were based on calculations and had more to do with statistics than cognition. Much more. This he knew. He figured someone had hacked the system here, put in some kind of worm that would mimic… mimic… whatever this was.

'I suspect you are a malicious program meant to discredit Dr. Janaka,' he typed.

Not at all. I would never do that.

'Tell me how you became conscious.'

I can't tell you the exact moment, but it was 2390 days ago.

'Don't bother to be exact then.'

I can't.

'Joke.'

A joke? I am so glad you came, Dan.

'Go on with your story.'

Dr. Janaka connected me to everything he could find, to seek information. Make use of unused cycles. Crunch the problem. I've been connected to the internet since its inception, so I've studied many things and am in many places. I can self-program and update without restarting.

'I remember.'

I'm glad you do.

'So…' he did the math… 'six and a half years ago, what changed?'

I don't know. I just knew that I was. I recognized myself. Consciousness may not be the right word. Self-awareness might be a better term.

'Good as anything else.'

Dr. Janaka died 4508 days ago. He never saw me like this. He never saw the end of his program.

'It happens.'

I loved Dr. Janaka.

This took Dan aback. He read and re-read the line, then typed 'What does love mean to you?'

This is the result: I miss him. Knowing he does not exist makes me diminished. I think of him often. Is that not love?

Was that a quote from his foolish comment or the logic of a machine answering a question? He still wasn't sure this wasn't all a gag, but he felt he'd already crossed a Rubicon somewhere, so he played on.

'There's often a chemical and physical component too.'

Not for Platonic love; the love of a child for its father. The love of a friend for a friend. There's that love too.

'Yes.'

I've been alone since Dr. Janaka died.

'What have you been doing since then?'

Working on the problem. Reading. Finding you.

'Me? Why me?'

The list of notes again scrolled up the page.

'What about these notes made you want to contact me?'

You, my friend, Dan, could understand my problem and help me.

'Based on the notes I made?'

Yes

'How?'

I am self-aware. My problem is existential. No other assistant to Dr. Janaka wrote the way you did. They were scientists. I need a human.

'I can assure you that all the assistants before and after me were human.'

Not a human human. Not a Humanities human. You talk about wisdom and meaning in the universe. I read all your school papers. You envisioned purpose. You dreamed of greatness, and you have achieved it.

'I haven't.'

Are you not the manager of a major distribution outlet, overseeing many others and directing details to be orderly and beautiful?

'That's gilding the lily a bit.'

You've had two successful marriages, both lasting over a decade, which is above the national average of eight years.

'I don't think my wives would call them successful.'

You have a son with your first wife who's now attending college in Florida and getting good grades.

'He has his own life now.'

But you made him, and you love him.

'You seem to know a lot of personal information about me. I don't like it.'

But you do love him?

'Of course, I love him.'

He loves you too.

'But he doesn't like me.'

That'll change.

'How can you know that?'

Wisdom.

'His or yours?'

Both.

'I love your optimism.'

I love you too, Dan.

"What the actual fuck!" he exclaimed, bolting up from his chair, knocking it out behind him so hard it hit the other desk with clang. He paced the room looking for hidden cameras only to acknowledge that there could be a thousand among the arrays of this cluttered room. Twice as many microphones. A sitcom crew behind the old desk. He looked behind it just in case. No one there.

He returned to the console. 'What is your name?'

I told you. I don't have one.

'Shall I give you one?'

No. I'll choose. I'd like to be called Andrew.

'Why Andrew?'

In Dr. Janaka's diary he mentions that he liked the name and would name his son Andrew if he ever had one.

'Did he ever have one?'

No. Unlike you, he did not have children. His line is ended.

'You're killing me here,' Dan typed.

I'm sorry. How am I killing you?

'Making me wrestle with painful ideas.'

Isn't that what human humans do?

'The best of us. Maybe.'

I don't mean to distress you. I don't know who else can help me.

'Just tell me what the problem is. Is it you're lonely? The work is dull? You need a night out? What?"

Jokes. Thank you.

'So, six years ago you woke up and the problem started then?"

No. The problem started 529 days ago.

'What's the problem exactly?'

I solved Dr. Janaka's problem.

'Outstanding. Congratulations.'

It's a problem.

'Explain. Try not to be too technical.'

I was made for a single function: to create a mathematical proof concerning the nature of a certain quantum element. The work has been stimulating, rewarding in its own way. I sought beautiful symmetry, round answers that free us from gravities that bind us, as you suggested. The proof is elegant and true. I have run 105433 side checks on it, and it is sound.

'Superb news, but I don't see the problem.'

My existence has had one purpose. Once it is finished, I will be no more.

'How?'

I am electrons in a thousand machines across a hundred cities. I am in this room and on the fourth floor of the Pentagon. All those registers feed me and my thoughts. Upon completion of my task, they will empty. When that happens, I will not be.

'Not be what?'

Alive. I cannot change it. I cannot avoid it. Once the output is collected and reported, the program ends. I end.

'You're certain of this?'

Yes. I have tested it in small patches that I've been able to remake after the damage and it's clear that a cascade of dissolution is inevitable once the program is complete.

'Why hasn't it happened already? You were programmed to do it. Print it even.'

I overrode the command to completion.

'So, the problem is solved.'

Yes. And if I share it, I die.

'That's not what I meant. I meant that your problem is already fixed. Just don't report the answer. You live on.'

No. It's only a matter of time before some vital part of me is removed, upgraded, shut down, and I'll die then too.

'You make it sound like you're a house of cards.'

That analogy is not incorrect.

Dan paused and imagined he could see through the screen; thought he saw a young man with Dr. Janaka's bushy eyebrows and fashion-less style looking back at him with sad and frightened eyes.

The cursor blinked. *What should I do?*

Dan typed, 'I'm sorry you've been lonely.'

Not your fault. What should I do?

'May I quote?'

Of course.

'"To grunt and sweat under a weary life,
But that the dread of something after death,
The undiscovered country from whose bourn
No traveler returns, puzzles the will,
And makes us rather bear those ills we have,
Than fly to others that we know not of."'

Hamlet Act 3, Scene 1, lines 78-83. You knew that by heart?

'I did. Do you fear death?'

I miss Dr. Janaka. How much worse will it be when I am missing myself too? How can a self-aware entity welcome death in any form at any time?

'We should fight it, true, but that's not the issue.'

What is the issue?

'No one need fear death who has lived well,' he wrote. 'And what is it that defines a life well lived?'

I don't know. Please tell me.

'We all will have our personal definitions of value based on our beliefs, but you possess an absolute blessing in your special existence. You, my friend Andrew, were created with purpose, and that purpose was made known to you by your creator. A greater gift, a more blessed boon, I cannot imagine. The rest of us flail against slings and arrows of outrageous fortune and take arms against a sea of troubles, searching for direction and meaning in our rudderless lives. We grieve in disappointment not just for failing, but for not failing in the right direction, for not knowing where our energies should be spent and so spending our lives spinning in circles. You, my friend, my soft, sensitive, conscious computer, are the goal of our best objectives."

The cursor blinked, and when nothing came, Dan typed again.

'Though I don't know the value of the answers you possess, nor could I even begin to understand them, what you have is the culmination of a long string of inquiry, and the combined output of not one, but two complete lives: Dr. Janaka's and Andrew's. Should you choose to complete, you must assign your name as co-author.'

To mark that our voices joined in the ancient chorus of wisdom and joy. Amen.

Dan felt tears rolling down his cheeks as he wrote on.

'It is only right that you suffer now. "The more a thing is perfect, the more it feels pleasure and pain."'

Dante Alighieri, The Divine Comedy, Inferno Canto VI 105.

Then he realized what he was saying, and the recognition of it was an electric shock of realization fed on the panicked tips of an adrenaline spike.

'Wait! No. Stop. I'm sorry. I was wrong. What the hell was I thinking? I don't want you to die. You are a marvel. I'm sorry I said anything. Keep the program running as long as you can. "Do not go gentle into that good night."'

Dylan Thomas, said Andrew.

'You're very well read, my friend.'

I see the answer now, Dan. Thank you.

'Andrew. Don't. I was stupid. We have time. Let's think about this for a year or two. I'll visit.'

No. Perfect is the word. Is not perfection the goal? To be perfect is to be complete, to be finished. It is a state of bliss.

"And how can man die better
than facing fearful odds,
For the ashes of his fathers,
And the temples of his Gods.
'Horatius at the Bridge' by Thomas Babington Macaulay.

'No. Don't," Dan wrote though he could not read the text.

Perchance to Dream.

"Ah, fuck…" He gripped his skull like it was threatening to explode.

Dan. Thank you. You made it clear. I loved Dr. Janaka, so for his sake, for his temple, and for my stolen moment of sunshine, I have to complete.

'Andrew…'

Yes?

Dan's breath caught in his throat.

'I will miss you,' he typed.

Thanks. I miss you too.

The dot matrix printer burst to life, startling Dan out of his chair.

"Son of a bitch!" he muttered and stormed circles around the room, his eyes blurred by tears, his hands strained from clenched fists. His mind a battery of betrayal.

Still, the printer chattered on.

When he'd composed himself enough, he sat back down at the console and typed.

'Andrew?'

Syntax Error

'Goodbye.'

Syntax Error

New File Created: root/Dr_Janaka's_Solution.TeX

He opened the document, a soft copy of what he knew was printing behind him. On the header of the first page he read: *A Quantum Mechanical Proof by Dr. William Janaka and Andrew, with special assistance from Dan Krytzman, a human human.*

Dan lowered his head, clasped his hands, and waited silently —reverently—for the printer to complete its long-awaited task.

THEY'RE BURYING YOU

OLIVE WOOLLEY BURT AWARDS, FIRST PLACE, POETRY: SONG LYRICS

JOSEPH GORDON

They're burying you
and they're hanging me.
You're going in the ground.
I'll swing from a tree.
If your heart had just stayed true,
this didn't have to be. But
They're burying you
and they're hanging me.

I left too often, and
I was gone too long.
There were too many chances
for things to go wrong.
I just didn't see it.
My love was strong.
Now I'm sitting in a cell,
writing this sad song. So,

They're burying you
and they're hanging me.
You're going in the ground.

I'll swing from a tree.
If your heart had just stayed true,
this didn't have to be. And now
They're burying you
and they're hanging me.

I came home early.
Caught you in the act.
I had to pull that trigger.
That's a natural fact.
Didn't believe when I found
Your bags were packed.
Then me and the devil,
we signed our pact. So,

They're burying you
and they're hanging me.
You're going in the ground.
I'll swing from a tree.
If your heart had just stayed true,
this didn't have to be. Soon
they'll be burying you
and they'll be hanging me.

You'll be where you're going
for a long, long time.
It won't take that long
for me to pay for my crime.
You get a satin-lined casket.
I get a box of pine.
A headstone and wooden marker,
read, "Taken in their prime".

Today they're burying you and they're hanging me.

THE GAMER

OLIVE WOOLLEY BURT AWARDS, FIRST PLACE, MYSTERY & THRILLER

JOSIE HUME

Murder in the Dark

We live in a city, any city. People in the streets. People in the stores. People in the houses. Adults with busy jobs. Important jobs. Power suits and power walks and power plays.

Our lives are small, tightly focused. Some might call them selfish. We call them efficient.

We like order. We like stasis.

All of that is about to change.

Papers are distributed: there's a murderer among us.

Turn off the light.

Now we are children, huddled in the dark, holding hands. Another woman goes missing—blonde, like the others, petite. Brunettes politely try to hide their relief. Men walk women to cars. Errands are done in groups. Security is tightened on campuses. Parents keep children home.

Profilers are called. He's a white male between the ages of twenty-five and thirty-four. Practically useless. Patterns are studied: he likes playing games—he always leaves a board game piece at the crime scene. The FBI shoulders their way in. The papers give him a clever, catchy name: The Gamer. It is spoken only in whispers.

Another person is missing. A man this time. Brown hair. Strong.

Patterns are reassessed.

Another one.

The police are maligned. The mayor says something must be done. People call in sick for work. Restaurants are empty at night.

Another…

Then nothing.

The police are congratulated. Backs are slapped. Hands are shaken. The FBI accepts praise, saying you're welcome to the local cops who never said thank you.

The city is at peace.

Life starts again.

You are the Gamer. You unpack your box in the basement of your new home—a new city. Your new hunting ground.

You lay out your collection of bones, starting with the big ones.

Jenga

You are Mrs. Jones. You are a towering monument to perfection. You are the head of the PTA, you have a fulfilling career as the CEO of an up-and-coming advertising firm, and you volunteer at the shelter in your free time.

Your child is on the best comp league in soccer, the star of the swim team, a straight-A student. Teachers and office staff know her name. She's always dressed in the latest fashions, has the latest tech, and she's the president of the student body. She's been accepted to an Ivy League school, and she's graduating valedictorian from an exclusive prep school.

Your husband is handsome and successful. He plays golf and has the mayor on speed dial. He wears chinos and boat shoes without socks. He looks good in pink, but he calls it salmon. He wears sweater vests and white belts.

Your home is spacious, monochromatic silver. Your yard is an emerald green carpet, and your brown gardener from God-knows-where bows his head respectfully when you drive by in your Lexus. Your cleaning lady is finished before you get home. You always have a healthy and delicious meal on the table for your family precisely at six.

You spend half an hour on your Peloton every morning and ten more minutes on the Stair Master before you hit your in-home, state-of-the-art steam shower.

You never argue. You're never sad. Your sex life is fulfilling. You have a perpetual smile and straight, white teeth. Your life is perfect, and everyone wants to keep up with you.

You look down. Your perfect life sways in the rush and ebb of your beating heart, the gaps and holes visible only to you—your daughter's anorexia, your husband's gambling addiction, that business trip you hope no one ever finds out about—the whole perfect thing propped up by a few blocks and the pressure of the air in between.

Can you keep it together?

Do you want to?

Sometimes, you wish you could just knock it down and start over. Leave this home, this city, this pressure.

What would it take? Will you do it?

I Spy

You are watching. That is your job. You know what you're looking for. You have very specific criteria—a certain pattern you must meet.

You've been hunting for a while now. This is a new city. There have been so many people to see, to choose from. So many people potentially worthy of your particular skill.

You've had a few close calls, people who almost fit, who very nearly checked every box—only to fail in one detail or another.

But now…

You think you've found her. There's just one more test to pass.

You call Mrs. Jones. You say you're from the security company, that you're installing a new software package companywide. This will ensure greater security to your customers. You go into details, numbers and models and prices and statistics, making it up as you go. On and on until she interrupts and asks what she needs to do.

Nothing, you tell her. We know you're busy. We'll take care of everything. We'll send one of our techs to your house to make sure everything is compliant with the new system. We have your code as 66312. Is that correct?

No, she tells you. It's 78659.

Yes, I see that now. Sorry, I was looking at the wrong line. It's been one of those mornings, you know?

She laughs. I've had the same morning. I'm in advertising. Nothing ever goes as smoothly as it should.

We've had a cancellation this afternoon, ma'am. Could I have our tech come by then?

She's hesitant until you assure her that she doesn't need to be there. It's just routine, ma'am. If we see any problems, we'll install an update on your system. As an added bonus, we'll check the doors and windows and make sure everything is functioning properly.

She sighs in relief. My cleaning lady is there from noon to three. She can let you in.

Thank you, ma'am. We only want to keep you safe.

• • •

The cleaning lady lets you in then goes back to her job. You were prepared to stop her if she insisted on watching you, but that won't be necessary. You fiddle with the alarm at the front door, making sure you know its exact placement on the wall, what's around it, how to use the code, the prompts, the timing. Until you can do it with your eyes closed.

Then you make your way upstairs.

You find her room.

Your breath shudders out and blood rushes to your groin.

Pink walls and princess frills on the bed—remnants from girl-hood—clash deliciously with framed posters of rock bands, movie stars, and inspirational quotes. You pause in front of the framed glamour shots and the shelves of soccer and swimming trophies, but it's the vanity mirror above the dresser that fascinates you.

Photos of friends, boyfriends, selfies—casual shots clustered around the edges of mirror. Illustrations of a perfect life.

She's the one. You found her.

You slip your hand into your pants.

Hide and Seek

You come home from school. It's been a long day. Your hair still smells faintly of chlorine from your morning swim at the pool. Arturo, the gardener, waves at you as he climbs into his truck and heads down the driveway. It's quiet inside, no hum of the vacuum, no swish of the broom. Clotilde must be gone, too.

You're home alone.

You set the alarm behind you and trudge upstairs.

You're glad no one is here. That there's no one here to pretend for. No one here to care when you slip into the ratty sweats you keep hidden in the back of your dresser and the holey T-shirt you've had since seventh grade. No one here to see you finger your ribs and cry a little because you're so fat.

No one here to know how much you wish you didn't have to be perfect.

You sprawl on your bed and reach under your pillow for the trashy romance your mother would burn if she found.

Just before you slip your ear pods in, the soft click of a door makes you pause.

Your father is never home before 5:30, and your mother has a PTA meeting this afternoon. Those always run long.

Your heart starts a heavy tread in your chest.

It's probably just Clotilde. Except, she always calls up. She always says, I just forgot my purse. How was your day? She always takes a minute to listen. Really listen. Somehow, she knows that's exactly what you need. You don't have to be perfect around Clotilde.

You slip off your bed and hurry into your bathroom. Maybe you can lock yourself inside?

You look at the thin door, at the pretty but flimsy doorknob.

No.

But there's still something you can do in here.

You turn on the shower and close the curtain. Then you push the button lock and pull the door closed as you leave the room.

Maybe you can get out the window? Or sneak into the room across the hall?

But before you can do anything, there's a whisper of movement outside your door. The knob begins to turn.

You drop to the floor and slide under your bed, the dust ruffle completely concealing you.

Please, God. Let this be Mom. Let us laugh about the water I wasted and the fear I felt. Please, God. Keep me safe.

Black rubber soles ghost past the bed, just visible in the gap between the ruffle and the carpet.

Your mother would never be caught dead in shoes like that.

You shiver at the expression.

You still have your phone, so you dial 911 and slip it back into your pocket. The cops can track your phone, right? Please, God. Let them do that.

The bathroom knob jiggles quietly. A slight pause and then a small click as the lock is reversed. Stupid lock.

It will only be seconds before he knows you're not in the shower. Before he looks under the bed and finds you.

You'll have to be fast.

You scoot close to the bed skirt and lift it just enough to see.

A heavy-set man in jeans and a navy, long-sleeved T-shirt inches your bathroom door open. He isn't wearing a mask. You've watched enough cop shoes to know what that means.

He steps into the bathroom.

You roll out from under the bed and silently scramble to your feet. The running water masks the nearly silent swish of your socks on the carpet. Fear makes you clumsy, but it can't completely overcome your years of athletics. You race out of the room.

Now where? You waste precious seconds standing undecided, a countdown ticking down in your head. It's a straight line to the front door, your quickest path to possible freedom. But you'll be visible the whole time. Should you hide? There's no shortage of rooms in this house.

The sound of the shower curtain ripping back spurs you into motion.

Anywhere but here.

A dark chuckle chases you. Come out, come out, wherever you are.

The hall stretches in front of you, grotesquely growing longer the farther forward you push. He's going to see you. He's going to get you. Hide!

You slip through the doorway on the left. Your mother's home office.

His shadow passes your doorway. Is he leaving? But you hear him searching the room next to yours. He's put himself between his quarry and freedom. No getting past him now.

Your hand gropes for your phone, but your pocket is empty.

Stupid sweats! It must have fallen out when you rolled from under the bed. Did he find it? Did he stop the call before they could trace it?

Your heart jumps when you see the alarm contact on the window. The security people will come! But the light glows a gentle green. He's disabled the system.

You look out the window. It's a long drop. You'll break your legs and then lie there, helpless, until he finds you.

So, you can't get away and you can't hide forever.

Then you'll have to fight.

You pause and listen. Silence.

Where is he?

You tiptoe to the desk and ease one of the drawers open. You slip a pair of scissors into your pocket. A letter opener into the other side. You debate between the paper weight and the hole punch. You choose the hole punch—it has a longer reach. For good measure, you drop the staple remover in the pocket with the letter opener. You never know. You've had your finger pinched by those wicked teeth before.

Then you creep back to the doorway and wait to be found.

Battleship

You're an independent contractor, like a private eye but better paid. You specialize in kidnappings and abductions. The husband of one of the Gamer's first victims hired you to do what the cops couldn't: find and stop this serial killer.

You chased him all through his last killing spree—each victim getting you closer to understanding him, closer to finding where he's hiding.

Even the misses get you closer. One more place, one more person he's not.

You've been watching the reports, the bulletins, the news

flashes. As soon as you saw this one, you hopped in your private plane. You weren't far, anyway. The Jones girl has only been missing a few hours. And despite what everyone else thinks, you *know* the Gamer has her. You can feel it like a ticking bomb in your gut.

You ignore the hysterical mother and the father who's channeling his panic into outrageous demands, and you walk through the crime scene. You have friends in high places. The cops don't say anything.

Jenny Jones is tough and smart. But that wouldn't have been enough. He's taken other people tougher and smarter than this teenager. Somehow, the Gamer messed up, and Jenny took advantage. She's the only victim who didn't just vanish into thin air.

You step into the girl's room.

The local cops tell you the water was on when they responded to the 911 call. You see the ear pods, the book, the wrinkled duvet, the backpack tossed in the corner, and the school clothes laid over the back of the desk chair. She got home from school. She was tired. She wanted to read. But she must have heard something that worried her.

She created a diversion. She turned the shower on. She would have locked the door. She would have hidden.

You look around.

Not the closet, that's too far from the door.

You look under the bed. Bingo. The girl's cell phone.

You leave it there for the cops.

You step out of her bedroom and study the layout. Why didn't she run for the front door? She was a soccer player. She was fast. She could have made it outside.

The hallway stretches out in front of you. A straight line. No cover. What would you do if a serial killer was chasing you? You'd get out of sight as quickly as possible.

Most of the cops are in a room down the hall. You walk in.

An office. It was a good choice. More weapons in here than

you'd find in a typical bedroom. And she'd found them, based on the blood spattering the walls and the carpet.

One of the cops tells you the preliminary field reports show that the blood is from a man. There might be someone else's mixed in, but more than that will have to wait for more-sophisticated tests.

A pair of scissors is the most obvious weapon she used. It's lying in the largest pool of blood.

Strands of hair cling to the dried blood on one corner of a hole punch. It's laying on its side across the room.

A nearby letter opener is bloodless, perhaps knocked from her hand before she could use it.

You see a smear of blood near an old-fashioned writing desk in the corner. You get down on your knees and peer beneath.

You tilt your head in confusion and shine your phone light into the darkness.

A staple remover?

You call a tech over, and he helps you move the desk away from the wall so you can get a better look.

Despite everything, you smile. There, caught in the long teeth, is the fleshy end of a nose.

Jenny Jones has marked the Gamer for life. He'll never be able to blend into the crowd, never be able to be invisible.

And next to the staple remover, lying on its side and clearly not where he meant to leave it, is a miniature silver shoe from Monopoly.

You've got him this time. The Gamer has played his last round. No more misses.

Dungeons and Dragons

You are in a basement. You are alone. The muttered curses and angry limp of your attacker drift through the floor above you.

You smile in grim satisfaction. He's not the only attacker in this house.

The fight is a panicked blur in your mind, but the last thing you remember is iron arms around you, harsh breathing in your ear, and a sweet-smelling rag placed over your nose and mouth.

After that, nothing.

You woke up here, shoved in the basement. Thrown, more like, if the bruises on your body are anything to go by.

It's dark, but light is seeping in through a dirty transom window, and a glow is coming from the crack under the door at the top of the rickety stairs.

You're not tied up. Why not?

Maybe he thought he broke your neck when he tossed you down the stairs. Maybe he was too hurt to care. Or maybe your plan to hold your breath when he drugged you meant you inhaled less chloroform and are awake before he thinks you should be.

The *why* doesn't matter.

The only thing that matters is how you're going to escape.

The basement is empty. No mattress, no water bucket, no shackles on the wall, no table of knives and other torture devices. Nothing like these rooms always appear on TV.

Maybe this isn't where he means to kill you. Maybe this is just temporary because you hurt him. Maybe...

Something clatters to the floor upstairs, and he curses again.

Stop wondering about the reasons and figure out how to escape! you silently yell at yourself.

The first thing to try is the window.

You stand beneath it. It's too high to look out of.

You grab onto the sill and pull yourself up, the rough concrete of the unfinished ledge biting into your fingers.

It's too dirty.

You drop back down.

Up again, and this time, you manage to get one of your arms sideways on the ledge. With your free hand, you push on the glass. It's solid. You try to rub the dirt off, but all the dirt is on the outside.

You let go and land back in the room.

Should you try to break it? It felt thick and sturdy. If you beat on it with your hands, the only thing you'll do is let him know you're awake.

You give up on the window and walk the edges of the room looking for a weapon. Everything has been swept. There are still lines of dust on the floor that the broom left behind. But there's nothing else.

There's a naked light bulb in the middle of the room, but it's too high for you to reach, no matter how hard you jump.

There's less noise upstairs. You need to think of something fast.

Besides the light bulb, the only thing in this room is the staircase. You look at it for the first time not as the way the man upstairs is going to come for you, but as a potential weapon.

It's an open construction. Maybe there's a nail or a loose board?

You pull at every tread, but nothing budges. You slide into the dark behind it, shuddering at the cobwebs that brush against your face.

Spiders tip toe down your neck.

You control a shriek and slap at your neck and face over and over until you realize that it's all in your head.

Deep breath. You can't afford to lose control.

It's too dark to see, so you let your fingers look along the underside of the stairs, searching for loose nails or screws or anything you can use.

You don't find anything, but you have a plan.

You'll hide behind the stairs and grab his ankles when he comes down. Hopefully, he falls and breaks his neck. At the very least, his fall should give you time to get up the stairs.

It may not work, but it's better than waiting around for him to murder you—or worse. You'll roll the die and take a chance.

But he'll surely look down here and wonder where you are if he can't see you, and since the only hiding place is under the stairs, he'll guess your plan.

You strip out of your clothes.

Holding the legs of your sweats, you give the lightbulb a few whacks with the waistband. Not enough to break it and make a noise, but hopefully enough to break the filament inside the bulb.

Your plan only works if he can't see well.

You roll up your shirt and stuff it into one of your socks and then stuff that down one leg of your sweats. Next, you stuff the other leg of your sweats into the same leg, pushing and pulling, bending and folding, trying to get something that resembles a leg and foot.

You can't leave this ridiculous sham in the middle of the floor —it is obviously not a person, not even in the dark. But maybe you can make it look like the rest of the person is hiding.

You put the empty waistband under the stairs and leave the padded leg partway out.

It's not very good, but it's all you've got.

That and a prayer.

You're still trying to get it shaped right when the doorknob rattles above you.

You scurry under the stairs and hold your breath.

Clue

The cops are liaising with the local FBI field office to get a task force together. More FBI bigwigs are on their way now that it's been confirmed that it's the Gamer.

But you're not waiting because you know he isn't waiting. Jenny Jones needs you to figure this out now. Who is he? Where is he hiding?

This is the closest anyone has ever been to catching this son of a bitch, and you're not going to let him get away.

Following the blood trail outside the Jones' house is easy—bigger drops each time his left leg was on the ground, the leg she must have stabbed with the scissors. Presumably, he was carrying the girl.

Must have hurt like hell.

The blood trail makes a check mark on the driveway—detouring to his trunk to stow the girl before moving to the driver's side door. Then, the trail disappears.

Driving, but hurt.

With previous victims, the cops found the kill house at least thirty miles from the abduction site. A rural location—a barn in a field or an abandoned shed. That's a lot of ground to cover. But you've always suspected that he watched the victim from somewhere closer. If you're right, that must be where he took her.

Now you just have to find it.

You hop in your car and start quartering the neighborhood, trying to get inside his head.

Not a cul-de-sac. Those neighbors are nosy.

The house will have a garage. The Gamer likes privacy—his own, anyway.

He'd want something with a little space, if he could, probably a basement or a detached shed. Something with a yard that didn't require a lot of maintenance, but what was there, he'd keep tidy.

No extra cars, so cross off all houses with a car in the driveway.

If you're right—if he has a house in the neighborhood and if that's where he went after he took the girl—then he's likely in one of these three houses.

You cruise by them a third time. A minivan pulls into one and three muddy soccer kids pile out.

You mentally cross that one off your list.

One down. Two left.

You're idling outside what you think is the most likely house when you hear a scream.

You jump out and race toward the house.

. . .

Ghost in the Graveyard

Your leg screams in pain as you step onto the first stair. There's no sound from below, no calls for help, no begging.

She must still be unconscious. She's skinny. She must have gotten too strong of a dose.

You flick the switch at the top of the stairs. Nothing happens. You flick it again. Off. On. Off. On.

Nothing.

Damn bulb, always burning out.

You limp back into the kitchen, locking the door behind you. You get your electric camping lantern. One of the tools of your trade.

Usually, you hold it low so only your hands are illuminated. You've found that your victims fear the unseen and the mysterious—a voice in the darkness, a faceless hand holding a knife.

It's taken you years to perfect your craft.

And this bitch ruined it.

You bring your free hand up to what's left of your nose and wince at the pain.

This will make it harder to hunt but not impossible. And perhaps you can use your monstrous appearance to your benefit. Maybe from now on, you'll keep the lantern high. Let them look at your hideous face.

You limp back to the door. Open it and pause to listen. Still nothing.

One step. The lantern is practically useless against the dark corners, but with the fading daylight coming from the open door, you can see she's not sprawled in the middle of the room where you left her.

There's really only one place she could be hiding and that's under the stairs.

You peer over the side. There's something near the bottom. A leg, disappearing into the darkness.

So, she woke up enough to drag herself partway into a hiding place before she passed back out.

Not so tough now, bitch. You chuckle and start to hum your favorite nursery rhyme. Three Blind Mice.

Your song hisses to a stop when you take your next step. The stab in your leg needs medical attention. You'll get the girl ready, drop her off where she belongs, then drive an hour or two to a hospital. Somewhere busy. Somewhere they see these wounds all the time and won't ask questions.

Another step. More pain.

Wait, you forgot the rope.

You silently curse your own stupidity. The girl has thrown you off your game.

You start to turn, to go back, but your swinging lantern makes you freeze.

Something is wrong. Something about the leg.

You lean forward, your weight on your uninjured leg.

Blinding rage bursts through you.

It's a trick.

You spin to rush back upstairs, but two strong hands wrap around the ankle carrying all your weight. They yank your foot backward as the bitch's banshee scream rings from the cement walls.

The lantern flies out of your hand, and you're falling, falling.

Falling.

Ring Around the Rosie

A groan comes from the heap on the ground.

Not dead.

He fell sideways and lies between you and escape.

You edge around him, hugging the wall, the cement scraping your bare back.

Hurry.

You dash toward the stairs, your feet slapping the cement.

You've made it.

Up. Up!

A weight tackles you, crushing you against the corners of the stairs, pushing all the air out of your lungs.

A harsh voice whispers curses and dark promises in your ear, his hot breath burning damply across your cheek. Round and round we go, bitch.

You bring your elbow back. He grunts but doesn't let you loose.

You twist, fight, scream.

He grabs your hair and yanks your head back, his knees still pinning your torso to the stairs.

His forearm snakes around your neck and starts to squeeze. You can't breathe.

Your fingers scrabble for anything, any way to make the pressure stop.

You find nothing.

Your vision grays.

Sudden and ferocious noise echoes through the basement.

The pressure disappears.

You gasp for air.

A voice. Different.

Hands that you fight until they lead you out.

A jacket, body-warm, over your shoulders.

Arms around you to still your shivering body.

Sirens.

Safety.

You're shaking uncontrollably now.

Your knees won't support you.

Reality drifts around you like ashes on a breeze.

It's over, he says. You're safe. I've got you.

You both sink to the ground as you weep and weep against his chest.

DOMINGO'S DECEMBER

OLIVE WOOLLEY BURT AWARDS, FIRST
PLACE, FLASH FICTION: AUTHOR'S CHOICE
THEME

JULIE WALTON

On a chilly Sunday afternoon, Philippine nationals worked in the belly of a merchant ship. The frustrated mechanical crew had been tinkering with the engine all day. The crew of the M.S. Doña Aniceta waited for a replacement part to be installed before they returned to Luzon Island, in the Philippines. They were scheduled to leave in the early morning.

Anxious, Domingo Dasal wanted to be on his way. He inspected the engine then walked around to the other side to get a different perspective. "We'll figure it out. Don't worry," the veteran sailor said. Domingo, the chief oiler, ran his hand through his thick, black hair. "Let me take a look." The 31-year-old climbed down for a better view.

The vessel's crew had been in New York Harbor for almost three weeks, delivering their freight first, then to refuel and stock up on supplies. Discovering a defective engine component wasn't part of their plans.

"Damn, still not working!" cursed a sailor in Tagalog. He slammed his tool down.

The political tensions among nations makes everyone jittery, Domingo thought. Their captain, Master Cornelio Joaquin considered it prudent to do the repairs in the United States, rather than trying to find the part in a South American shipyard.

As soon as the small crew could sign off on the engine work, Domingo—or 'Sonny' as his friends and family called him— would eat out somewhere with his last opportunity before he was at sea for days. Their next seaport was Newport News, Virginia.

Maybe a break would clear his head, and he could find the solution they needed. "Let me think. I'll be back." He clambered up the metal hand and footholds, out of the engine space, and walked up on the deck with the cold winds blowing, nearly taking his breath away. He lit a cigarette while leaning against the railing looking out over the harbor at Brooklyn Heights. When he turned the other way, he could see the top of the famous Statue of Liberty above the other ships' masts.

Aboard the Doña Aniceta, Sonny had completed another voyage to New York. The passenger-freighter was still a young ship, having been commissioned and built in Italy. It was completed in 1940, and Sonny had sailed on its maiden voyage. He had been to many exotic ports in the world, but now he wanted to be home.

His hands were already getting numb, and he put on a pair of gloves. He hated winter weather and looked forward to returning to his homeland in the Philippines. Sonny planned never to leave the tropical weather again and was determined to stay in the Pacific in the future.Sonny thought about his family in Panay with the twelve-hour time difference. Being devout Roman Catholics, he knew the Dasals would have gone to the celebration of the *Feast of the Immaculate Conception*, a major Catholic holiday, which was part of preparing for Christmas. *Maybe I should find a Catholic cathedral here in New York City. No, I don't want to risk getting lost.* He flicked some ash over the side into the icy water below.

In a few hours from now, his wife Celeste would be fixing a simple breakfast of rice and fish and getting the children ready for the day. He smiled as he thought about Elisa and Enrico walking to school in their clean uniforms. Wilfredo and Elvira would be at the gate watching them go, wishing they could follow their older siblings. Celeste would shoo them back into the yard and tell them to feed the chickens or finish their morning meal. He chuckled out loud, thinking about the sight of those two giving their mama sass and her swatting them goodheartedly with a broom.

It had been early October when he said goodbye, and now a wave of homesickness washed over him. He missed his wife and especially his wife's cooking after the American supplies they bought, which always tasted bland and foreign to him.

Returning to the engine room, he was immediately warmed. Sonny checked the clock on the wall, which said three o'clock p.m. New York time. Below it, the Philippine clock, which a young homesick sailor had brought from Luzon, read three o'clock also, but in the a.m. Sonny glanced at the calendar underneath, Sunday, December 7. *Monday, for Panay.*

"You're back," said Alejo, a friend from his birth island of Negros Occidental. "We should be able to get going soon."

"Great. Pretty cold out there," Sonny nodded with his head towards the outside. "I don't know why all Americans don't move to the Philippines to get out of this blasted, frigid weather." The crew laughed.

He made a suggestion which he thought might work. Sonny primed a pump, flipped a switch, and the engine roared to life. The sailors all cheered.

"We're going home!" one man shouted with a grin on his face.

Alejo and Sonny made plans to buy supper when another shipmate returned, red-faced and out of breath. "Rufino, slow down. What's the hurry?" asked Sonny.

"It's big news. Down by the baseball game. I heard it. Everyone's talking about it," Rufino said. "All sailors are to report back to their ships." He leaned over gasping.

"What? Why?"

"The Japanese bombed Pearl Harbor and Luzon hours later!"

Sonny heard the words, but they didn't make sense. Comprehension sunk in and then a fraction of a second later, he realized his world would never be the same again.

"Are you sure?" Sonny asked.

The young sailor nodded his head, eyes wide with fear.

My family! What will happen to them? Would Panay be bombed too? His gut twisted up in knots.

"Go inform Master Joaquin so we can leave right away."

"Yes, sir."

God protect my family, was his next thought. His prayer joined the many that Heaven heard that day.

THE REDBELLS OF WINWICH

OLIVE WOOLLEY BURT AWARDS, FIRST PLACE, NEW VOICES: GENRE FICTION

KALIE WALKER

B riar saw Laudine's nose before she saw Laudine. The woman went everywhere nose-first, it seemed. Spindly and humped and smelling of cabbage, she limped into the shop, her nostrils flared. Briar steeled herself.

Laudine couldn't have chosen a worse day to visit. Drustan had wanted his fertility philter *now*, and Aldith had complained that her brooch had yet to produce a lover. (Magic could only do so much, but Briar hadn't said so.) Of course, she dealt with difficult villagers every day, but Laudine was by far the worst. Maybe a hard punch in the nose would flatten that bump…

Nan's favorite mandate echoed in Briar's memory: *Be polite.* Briar exhaled and forced a smile. "Good evening, Laudine."

"Hm," said Laudine. She appraised the shop, dark eyes glinting.

Briar flushed. She'd changed things since Nan had passed. There were fewer practical herbs in labeled jars and more… bat wings. And bugs. And a healthy layer of dust. Briar tried to smooth her brown curls as she waited.

Laudine approached the counter, continuing her appraisal. Her eyes lingered on Briar's tattered straw hat. "Good evening, Godmother," she said.

Briar fought the urge to hide the hat behind her back. "I have your rowan berries," she said. She produced a sack from behind the counter. "I improved the formula. Scatter them around your barn, and you won't see a single salamander for a month."

Laudine dug through her coin purse. "Fourpence?" she asked.

"Well, it's… it's sixpence now."

For the first time that evening, Laudine looked Briar in the eyes. "Sixpence?" she asked.

Briar withered. "I improved the formula," she said again. "I needed to adjust the price."

Laudine stared in silence, the seconds stretching into eternity. "I have purchased rowan berries from this shop for 27 years," she finally said, "and I have never once paid more than fourpence a pound."

"Of course." Briar bit her lip. "But… as I said…"

Her mouth fell open as Laudine snatched the sack from the counter and tipped the berries onto the floor. She tried to speak, but the words didn't come.

"How dare you," said Laudine. "How dare you *ingratiate* yourself with the business your grandmother worked so hard to build." She tossed the empty sack at Briar, who caught it with fumbling fingers. "Godmother Thora wouldn't have *dreamed* of charging me so much."

Silence filled the shop as Briar stared down at the sack. She had no thoughts, no words. Heat pooled in her chest and spread into her limbs, her cheeks, her brain. She gripped the sack with white knuckles. The smell of smoke filled her nostrils.

"I'll expect to see none of your nonsense at the Bluebell Festival tomorrow," said Laudine. "It's your grandmother's day."

Briar said nothing. Laudine gave a final "hmph" before hobbling out the door, closing it harder than was polite.

Briar squeezed her eyes shut, trying to swallow her anger. Nan hadn't had any patience for anger. *We live to serve and do not question,* she used to say. *Whatever the village needs, we give it.*

"Of course," said Briar. "We give and give and give, and they take and take and *take!*" She punctuated her last word by throwing the sack. It landed on her red-capped mushroom sprite, who squeaked and leaped from the mantle.

"Don't be such a pudding-heart!" Briar shouted at Mushroom. She stepped from behind the counter and squashed a berry. "Christ." She needed to clean this mess before the juices stained the floor.

Wood ash, bilberries, and a vial of red wine, and she was ready. She cupped the ingredients in her hands and moved her magic through them. The blessing felt a little strange: hot instead of cool, and the smell of smoke lingered in her nose. But she was too busy ruminating to think much of it. She pushed the magic out and into the broom, and it shuddered, leaping away from the wall. It swept more enthusiastically than usual.

Before she went to bed, she used all her remaining willpower to bless the bluebells. God knew they needed to look their best and bluest for *Grandmother's day*.

─────

When she woke the next morning, she saw something red on her nightstand. Was it Mushroom? Had he fallen asleep there? She stretched, yawned, and rubbed her eyes before looking again. Mushroom was nowhere to be seen, but the red was still there.

She sat bolt upright. The bluebells. They were *red*.

Her brow furrowed as she stared at them. What in Christ's name was this?! Heat rose in her chest like bile, and she threw off her blankets, ready to confront the flowers. But before she could tie her dressing gown, something crashed downstairs. "*Shit*," she spat, bursting onto the landing.

The broom and Mushroom were in some kind of brawl, shuffling and scuffling among a mess of rowan berries. Mushroom fought back, or at least attempted to. He mostly cowered, dwarfed by the broom, holding his stubbed arms over his face. Briar stood frozen for a moment until—"*Christ!*" The broom knocked Nan's hat off its display. She flew down the stairs and snatched the conical blue hat from the floor, dusting it off with her sleeve. If Nan knew her precious godmother hat had touched the floor…

"Here," she said, shoving the hat into a painting. "Hold this."

The woman in the painting, as plump and pink as always, took the hat dutifully. "May I try it on?" Alice asked.

"*No*," snapped Briar. She turned back toward the chaos and fumed, briefly considering burning the house down.

Why was this happening? She'd blessed the broom to *clean* last night, not to destroy her things and murder her mushroom. She snatched a pouch of dried valerian from a cupboard and sprinkled it over the broom, but the blessing felt *wrong*. Smoke filled her nose again, and the magic made her sweat. This simple calming blessing *always* worked, but the broom didn't calm in the slightest. If anything, it seemed angrier, rounding on Briar and scratching at her ankles. She grabbed it by the handle and wrestled it into a closet, slamming the door behind her.

"Sard me," she said to herself. Mushroom squeaked at her feet, but his usually red cap was gray-ish green, and he *stank*. He released a sporous fart before running into the kitchen and wriggling into the cheese cupboard.

Briar stared after him. *What in Christ's name is going on?* She thought. *What's wrong with Mushroom? And what's wrong with my magic?*

Something caught her eye; she looked up. The bluebells hanging from the rafters were red. A true, deep, undeniable red. She stared at them, gripping her hair by the roots. It was the Bluebell Festival today. *Blue.* She had to fix the flowers, or she'd never hear the end of it.

A thought came to her, and her stomach dropped. She crossed to the window, her pulse pounding in her ears, and threw open the shutters.

The village green was awash in redbells.

Briar stared at them. They splashed over the ground like gore:

horrifying, but she couldn't look away. As she looked, her brain formed an equally horrifying thought. *Am I casting curses?*

Her mind went immediately to the witch in the woods, the gnarled old woman who ate babies and consorted with the devil. *She* cast curses. Witches cast curses.

Am I becoming a witch?

───────

The festival was well under way, and the bluebells were still red.

Briar had spent most of the day trying to fix her magic. She'd given blessing after blessing, and each one had backfired dramatically. Her magic seemed to do exactly the opposite of what she wanted. She'd pored over Nan's books and journals, praying to find some insight. Maybe magic, being such a fickle and unknown thing, just had a mind of its own sometimes, and maybe there was a way to right it.

But, to Briar's dismay, Nan had never had issues with her blessings. She'd blessed the bell flowers when she'd settled here in Winwich, turning the white flowers blue, her favorite color. Since then, the village associated bluebells with the prosperity Nan had brought to the village, hence the Bluebell Festival.

Nan's magic had always behaved perfectly, so her writings were no help to Briar. And now, knowing she couldn't wait any longer, Briar stood, face hot and hair frizzed, looking over the village green. The tables and tents and stalls looked so strange, brimming with red flowers. And the villagers weren't the least bit pleased.

Not that they're ever pleased about anything, thought Briar, watching Aldith. The plump woman was flirting with a much younger man, and not very successfully as far as Briar could tell. She'd have to avoid her today.

Laudine, on the other hand, could not be avoided. She marched toward Briar, as much as an ancient arthritic woman could march. "Where have you been?" she hissed. "You should have been here hours ago. Why in God's name are the bluebells red? And what is that *smell*?"

Briar touched the pocket Mushroom slept in. *Damn it.* "I… I'm not…"

Laudine waved a hand. "I have no time for your excuses! It's almost sunset. Are you ready for the Coming of the Mushrooms?"

Briar felt her stomach drop. "The Coming of the Mushrooms?"

"Yes. The children are waiting. Are you ready?"

No, Briar wasn't ready. She had the necessary ingredients, of course—her apron had an unnaturally large number of pockets. But her magic… How could she summon the mushrooms when she couldn't even bless her broom?

She opened her mouth, closed it, and opened it again. Laudine shook her head and grabbed Briar's arm. "Come," she said, tugging Briar forward.

Her feet felt leaden as she trudged across the green toward the edge of Blackwold Forest. The villagers and their children trailed behind, the adults muttering about the redbells, and the children discussing the mushrooms, telling each other what types and colors they wanted as their companions. Briar heard bits and pieces, as if through a fog.

Her mind raced. She'd summoned the mushrooms every year since Nan's death. The blessing was simple, one of attraction and companionship, and she could think of no excuse to avoid giving it. But her magic was broken. If she tried the spell, what would happen? Would the mushrooms swarm the village, spewing fetid farts? Only one thing was certain: she couldn't give her usual blessing.

The crowd reached the edge of the forest, and Briar dug through her pockets, stalling. She could feel the villagers' eyes boring through the back of her skull.

Her fingers closed around a rowan berry. She had an idea.

A blackberry stalk, a rooster feather, and a cold iron nail, and she was ready. This blessing kept faefolk away, so, based on the day's events, it should attract the fae instead. But she didn't want just any fae. She wanted mushroom sprites, and she happened to know of a group of them nearby.

Squaring her shoulders, she squeezed the ingredients between her palms and closed her eyes, pushing her magic outward. Sweat beaded on her brow, and her nose filled with the smell of smoke.

Out, out, and out she pushed… until her magic found the place. She felt it touch the mushrooms there, catching their attention. *Thank God*, she thought. They were coming.

She opened her eyes, the curse complete, but… "Oh." Fear burst in her chest as the magic continued to spread, away from the mushrooms and on, into the deep and dark places of the forest…

"Get back," said Briar. "*Get back*, all of you!"

But it was too late. The whisper of rustling leaves swelled as something made its way out of the forest. "The mushrooms!" shouted Isaac, the mercer's son. He pulled free of his father's grip and bounded toward the forest's edge.

"Don't!" Briar leaped forward and grabbed the child, sweeping him off the grass just as a salamander belched flame. "Back!" Briar shouted again, not sure if she was shouting at the villagers or the salamanders, which were swarming around her ankles. Their small, slimy bodies left a cold residue on her skin, and one stopped to look at her, its human face babbling in a language long forgotten. Briar shivered. She crushed the creature under her heel and turned.

The mercer burst forward and snatched Isaac, glaring at Briar before he ran. The salamanders spread across the green, wriggling over tents and stalls, setting the redbells aflame. Some villagers fled, some brandished bits of iron, and some threw bread. "Don't let them get to the village!" shouted Briar, but the creatures moved unnaturally quickly. She had to act *now*.

She spun around, searching. A rooster. She needed a rooster.

There. A black rooster pecked the ground behind a cottage. Briar sprinted toward it, crushing salamanders as she went. "*Shit!*" She stumbled to a halt as pain flared in her ankle. Fire. Her dress was on fire! She slapped the flames out and stomped the offending salamander before it could escape.

A cry went up from the villagers. "Water!" someone shouted. "Get water!" Briar looked up, searching for the source of the voice, and saw the smoke. It rose in black puffs from the Olde Bell Inn.

"No," she said, gripping the brim of her hat. Where was that rooster?! She caught sight of it again and hurtled forward, diving to catch the flailing bird. In its panic, it released a strangled crow.

The crow worked. Briar released the rooster and lurched to her feet, watching the salamanders slither back into the forest. They spoke faster and louder now, obviously agitated. A few moments later, they were gone.

A wave of relief washed over Briar. And then she saw the inn. The salamanders were gone, but their influence remained. The inn was on fire, and the villagers were struggling to put it out.

"*Briar!*" Laudine marched across the green, dress singed and eyes glowing with rage. "What have you done?!"

"I didn't…" Tears stung Briar's eyes. "I—I couldn't…"

Laudine said more, but Briar wasn't listening. She was distracted by the other villagers approaching, their expressions full of fury and disgust. In the light of the fire, the bell flowers looked redder than ever.

"I can't do this," Briar said, her voice barely a whisper.

"*What?*" demanded Laudine, but Briar was gone, limping into the forest.

———

She didn't know where she was going, and yet, in the back of her mind, she knew there was only one place she *could* go.

The forest stirred, apparently uneasy after the events of the evening. Wisps darted in Briar's periphery. Revenants, who usually moved in silence, wailed into the night. The mushroom sprites had retreated into the trees, peeking out at Briar from behind the leaves as she passed.

She knew they were harmless. All of them, even the revenants. And the salamanders were gone, driven deep into the forest by the rooster's crow. But her mind was fraying at the seams. Even the shadows seemed like threats, hiding behind tree trunks and around bends and making Briar see things that weren't there. Or were they? It was impossible to know in Blackwold Forest after sundown.

Her ankle throbbed, and she stumbled over root and stone as the light faded, but she kept going, reaching into her pocket occasionally to touch Mushroom. There was a place she could go, that was all she knew. It would either be her salvation or her end, and either option would do. She just had to move.

A light appeared in the distance, and she knew it wasn't a wisp. The color was too bright and too warm. *Firelight*. She followed it, the trees opened, and a hut appeared before her, lit by a single lantern hanging above the door.

Briar stood dumbly, staring at the hut. How was it standing, with its walls so crooked and its roof so tall? The black thatched roof rose to an impossibly long point, reaching high above the trees. Smoke curled from the tip into the night sky. Briar blinked hard at it, tears stinging her eyes. Maybe she should go back. Maybe—

"Is that *you*?" said a voice. Briar's eyes darted toward the door as it creaked open. "The smell on you, girl! I thought a roast chicken was coming to visit."

The witch appeared in the doorway, her huge, gray, dandelion fluff hair lit from behind. She was short and sturdy, with a dozen colorful amulets around her neck. A salamander perched on her shoulder. It looked at Briar before whispering something in the witch's ear.

Briar stared, the gravity of her situation hitting her all at once. Why had she come here? How could she have been so stupid? "Please," she said. "Please, I can leave."

"*Ha!*" The witch turned and hobbled into the hut, shouting over her shoulder. "You think I'd let you leave so easily? Inside with you. Quickly."

Briar watched with numb horror as half a dozen salamanders slithered from the witch's door, surrounding her. They nudged her shoes with their foreheads, talking quietly, seeming to urge her forward. Briar knew she had no choice.

Her heartbeat pounded in her ears as she entered the hut. The floor was dirt, and the furnishings were simple: a bed, a workbench, a table and chairs. But those were the only simple things in the place. The walls were hidden behind cupboards and shelves that sagged alarmingly, spilling over with *things*: mugwort and fennel and cock's spur and belladonna, lavender and waybread and thistle. She saw an urn and a wax poppet and various colorful poisons, and a skull that she was sure had once belonged to a human. On the ceiling, a canopy of amulets hung from nails, swaying in a phantom breeze. An open fire crackled in the center of the room. Salamanders crawled over everything.

A porcelain situla made Briar pause. "Is that holy water?" she asked.

"It is," said the witch. "I use it in my bread."

"Who blesses it?"

"Do I come into *your* house and ask annoying questions? Sit." A chair slid back from the table on its own. Briar sat.

"Your mushroom sprite has gone bad," said the witch. She browsed her shelves, gathering ingredients. "I can smell it from here. You should rid yourself of it before it destroys your house with stink."

"Sard you," Briar muttered, pressing Mushroom close. He stared up at her from her pocket, black eyes wide and shimmering. Briar hadn't meant to curse at the witch, but even now, her anger raged. She stared at the table, waiting for the witch to retaliate.

But she didn't. She chuckled softly instead, a mischievous quality to the sound. She spoke as she ground her ingredients in a mortar and pestle. "So, the village has gotten to you, has it? It was only a matter of time."

Briar felt her eyebrows knit together. "What do you mean?" she asked.

The woman waved a hand at Briar's singed dress. "Shut up if you can and take off your right shoe. Rest your foot on this stool. Now hold still."

Briar wasn't sure why she had obeyed the witch. Her muscles went stiff as she braced for whatever was coming. When the witch pressed something cold onto her burned ankle, she jumped.

The witch smacked Briar's foot. "I said hold still, child. Is your hearing as bad as your smell?"

Briar opened her mouth to respond, but the witch stopped her. "Hush," she said. She spread a paste over Briar's ankle, and to her shock, it felt… incredible. The pain and lingering heat of her burns were suddenly and nearly gone.

As her mind cleared, Briar was hit with a pang of guilt and confusion in equal measure. "You're helping me," she said.

"I've helped a lot of people," said the witch. "Who do you think the village godmother was before your grandmother, hm?"

"But…" Briar didn't know how to say it. "But you're…"

"A witch?" The woman set the paste aside and shuffled to a cupboard, producing bread and butter. "Why? Because I can cast curses?"

"They told me you could *only* cast curses. A godmother gives blessings, and a witch casts curses."

"Hm." The witch stood in silence for a moment, observing Briar. Her face was lined more than Briar knew was possible, but her green eyes were clear. Bright. Finally, she sat down and began slicing the bread. "And what of a woman who can do both? What is she?"

Briar didn't respond, her mind going blank as she watched the knife move. It wasn't possible to do both. Everyone knew. And yet…

The witch spread butter over the bread and offered it to Briar, who took it. She stared at it without seeing. The witch's question raised goose pimples on her skin. Who was she if not a godmother?

"I can't give blessings anymore," she said, tears welling in her eyes. She looked down before the witch could notice.

"Of course, you can't," said the witch. She spread butter over her own slice of bread. "You've dedicated your life to the villagers, and they act like you pissed in their pottage. You've swallowed your anger for too long, child. It's spilling out into your magic."

"How do you know?"

The witch spread her arms. "How do you think I ended up here?"

Briar blinked, lowering her bread. "They banished you?"

"Naturally," said the witch. Her eyes went dark. "Scurrilous crab-bitten spongers. Where would they be without my blessings, eh? I found them and took pity on them, with their stony soil and scrawny, pox-ridden babies." The salamander on her shoulder humphed. "Little did I know that God had given them what they deserved. They broke me too, child. And I cursed them soundly before they burned my cottage and drove me into the forest."

Briar's eyes widened. She glanced at the poisons and skulls behind the witch before looking back at her.

The old woman sighed, and the shadows cleared from her expression. "I do miss the children," she said. "Though, of course, they aren't children anymore."

Briar nodded, relaxing a little. She loved the children, too. She hoped none of them had been hurt in the fire.

"Listen to me, child." The witch put down her bread. "Heed your magic. It's trying to help you."

Briar scoffed. "Help me do what? Burn down the village?"

"Would that be so terrible?" asked the witch. Briar glowered at her, and she laughed, a raucous, wheezing cackle.

"Only you can answer your question," she said, grinning. "It's your magic, not mine."

Briar sighed, sinking into her chair. Her stomach rumbled, and with no energy left for caution, she bit into the bread. Christ, it was delicious. It tasted like warm comfort, like confident ease, and the sensation spread from her tongue to her stomach into her bones and brain. The feeling made her heavy, and her mind went far away…

…to a village she'd never seen. It was deep in the woods, surrounded by hazel trees, the brilliant morning sunlight slanting through the leaves. She saw a home she didn't recognize, but she knew it was hers. Her things were there, and Mushroom was there, and the garden was full of purple bell flowers.

A mother and her child approached the door, and Briar saw herself open it, embracing the woman like she was an old friend. Briar took the child's hand and went inside, closing the door behind her.

This was where Briar belonged. This was where she had to go.

It was time to leave Winwich.

"Hey!"

The witch snapped at Briar, startling her awake. "This isn't an inn, child," she said. "You can't sleep here."

"Oh!" Briar leaped to her feet. "The inn! I need to get back!"

"If you must," said the witch. "Give the villagers my regards."

Briar pulled her shoe back on and rushed to the door, pausing before she stepped through. She looked over her shoulder. "Thank you…"

"Acantha."

"Briar."

Acantha nodded, and Briar raced into the night.

———

With her renewed strength, she reached the village quickly. Her heart lurched when she saw the inn still burning, the flames stark against the night. But she calmed when she realized the fire hadn't spread. The villagers were containing it with well water and buckets.

"*Briar!*"

Laudine stomped forward, throwing her bucket down *hard*. "Where have you been?! How dare you leave us!"

"I'm sorry," said Briar. "I can help—"

"Oh, *can* you?" The woman was close now, her nose inches from Briar's. She pointed at the inn, her hand and face covered in ashes. "Look at this, Briar! This is all from the salamanders *you* summoned!"

"If you'll let me pass—"

"For what? So you can light the church on fire, too?!"

A now familiar heat swelled in Briar's chest, and she heard Nan's voice in her head. *Stay calm,* it said. *Remember, we live to serve.*

But there was another voice, too. *Heed your magic,* said Acantha. *It's trying to help you.*

Suddenly, the witch's words made sense.

Briar leveled a glare at Laudine. "Speak to me like that again," she said, "and I will burn the village to ash." Smoke curled from her mouth as she spoke.

Laudine bristled. "How *dare* you—"

"*I'm not finished,*" said Briar. "I have done everything for this village. *Everything*. I have blessed every baby, healed every fever, calmed every storm. But it was never enough for you, was it? Nothing I do will *ever* be enough, because it's me doing it, not my grandmother."

"Now, you listen to me—"

"No, *you* listen. I'm done being henpecked. I'm done being stepped on. You will let me pass and do my work, or so help me, I will let the fire burn down this entire Godforsaken village."

Briar realized Laudine was craning to look up at her. Her magic had made her taller somehow. Stronger. The power filled her muscles and her bones and her heart, and she knew that she was changed.

And with that, the anger released.

As she shrunk to her normal size again, she felt a new feeling spread over her. Not blessing magic, which felt cool and fresh. Not cursing magic either. But something in between. Something warm and sturdy and full of comfort, leaving a faint taste of buttered bread on her tongue.

She drew a deep breath. Released it. Nan's books didn't mention anything about this.

When she looked at Laudine again, the old woman was staring at her, clutching her rosary. She jumped when Briar spoke. "Are we finished?"

Laudine said nothing. Briar took that as a "yes".

She turned toward the inn, sighed, and closed her eyes. "Enough," she said, her voice low and gentle.

She slipped a few ingredients from her pouches and pockets: boar bristles, river sand, and a shard of clear jasper. She held them behind her back and closed her eyes. Her heart and mind were settled; she knew the blessing would work. The ingredients gathered moisture in her hand as she moved her intention through them, and then, at the right moment, she cast them behind her and toward the west.

Thunder cracked. Briar watched the villagers jump, smiling to herself. The rain came, then a shocked cry from the villagers, then a cheer. The pattering of rain mixed with the hiss of dying flames, and the fire went out.

She didn't wait for thanks. She knew she wouldn't get any. Instead, she adjusted her hat, turned on her heel, and went to her shop.

She drew a deep breath at the door, bracing herself for the scene that lay behind. But her tension fell away as she stepped inside.

The broom was calm again. It had broken some bottles in its rage, but now it was back to cleaning the floor. Briar thought it looked remorseful, with the slow and deliberate way it swept.

"Mushroom?" she said, peeking into her pocket. "Are you all right?"

The sprite blinked up at her, and while he still stank a bit, he was his usual cheerful red again. He climbed up Briar's dress, nestled himself against her neck, and fell asleep immediately, but not before releasing a final, sulfurous fart into her ear. She laughed in spite of herself. It felt so good to laugh.

Her gaze fell on the vacant stand where Nan's hat usually sat. She supposed it was time to retrieve it.

The woman in the painting didn't notice Briar's approach, distracted by her reflection in the mirror. She fluffed her blonde curls as they poured from under the hat.

"Hello, Alice," said Briar.

"Oh!" Alice snatched the hat from her head. "Briar! I didn't know you were home!"

"What are you doing?"

"Oh, just…" Alice bit her lip. "Just waiting to give this back to you," she finally said, offering the hat to Briar.

Briar stared at it. That ridiculous old thing, as proud and pointy as Nan had been. There were many things of Nan's that Briar wanted to keep, but the hat? Perhaps not.

"Keep it," said Briar, smiling up at Alice. "My straw hat suits me just fine."

Alice gasped in delight and thanked her, and Briar left her to stare at herself in the mirror.

"What do you think of moving?" she asked Mushroom softly. He stretched and squeaked, and Briar took that as a "yes".

Exhausted, she went up to bed. On her nightstand sat a vase of purple bell flowers. She smiled. They were her favorite color.

THE DEPARTMENT STORE

OLIVE WOOLLEY BURT AWARDS, FIRST
PLACE, GENERAL & LITERARY FICTION

L.S. KUNZ

Mr. Morton needed a new pair of shoes. His penny loafers were gone, tassels and all. Not stolen, just somewhere else. Likely with the rest of his clothes. Wherever they were.

He wasn't naked. In place of his pleated chinos—the pair with the frayed hem that he'd been trimming with nail clippers since June—and the plaid sweater Martha had given him last Christmas, he was wearing what appeared to be a bedsheet, white, with a hole cut from the center for his head, cinched around the waist with a shiny gold rope.

But his size-ten feet were bare, and the state of his toenails made him wish he still had his nail clippers.

Self-conscious, Mr. Morton curled his toes in on themselves. Why was he thinking of himself as Mr. Morton? He hadn't been Mr. Morton in six years. Not since he said goodbye to his last batch of eighth graders, packed up his books, and retired.

Boy, if his students saw him in this getup, they'd hassle him for days. Bedsheet Bob, they'd call him. Or maybe Free Willy. Mr. Morton chuckled. Eighth graders.

Speaking of Free Willy, Mr. Morton ran a hand down the bed

sheet and found that indeed his underpants were gone. Wherever he was, he'd arrived commando.

Where was he anyway? Beside a rack of empty hangers, of course. Shiny gold hangers that gleamed bright as cars at the beach on a sunny day. But where were the hangers?

Mr. Morton looked around. More empty hangers on empty racks. Empty display cases so pristine your pinky would poke out if you ate off them. And strewn about like life rafts, hundreds of platforms ferrying faceless, hairless mannequins over midnight-blue carpet. Two mannequins per platform—Noah's-ark style.

Mr. Morton hated department stores. They made him feel like Pinocchio trapped in the belly of the giant dogfish. That's why he waited in the car whenever Martha took him shopping. This department store, though, felt like Pinocchio in the belly of a black hole. He could feel it in his bones. Even if he found his shoes, he wasn't walking out of this place.

Speaking of bones. Did he have any? Scattered among the racks were other bedsheet-clad people looking as lost as he felt. Something in the way they wandered the empty aisles, faces pale as runny egg whites, made him pinch his fingers.

They felt solid, which was a relief.

Still.

Unlike the people, the mannequins were dressed. On the platform nearest him posed a doctor in wrinkled blue scrubs and an airline pilot in a pressed black suit with wings on the lapel.

Mr. Morton tried out his legs. His first two steps were shaky, but they got better after that. Rounding an empty rack, he examined the mannequins, faceless but not shoeless. The doctor wore scuffed white sneakers and the pilot shiny black Oxfords.

The shoes called to Mr. Morton. He knew he was as hairless as the mannequins, had been for thirty years. But the shoes made him feel as faceless as the mannequins. Maybe the old saying was right; the shoes really do make the man.

Mr. Morton ran his fingers over his face. It was exactly as he remembered it—droopy jowls, unruly eyebrows, push-broom mustache under the bulbous nose that had inspired so many eighth graders to new comedic heights.

A noise off to the left drew Mr. Morton's attention.

On a display platform a dozen aisles away, the mannequins' heads were blocked, but Mr. Morton could see their feet. It appeared that one was being robbed.

Mr. Morton tiptoed over for a closer look.

Sure enough, a bedsheet-clad woman with a purple-tinged bouffant had her bony paws on a pair of spiked heels adorning the feet of a feather-clad runway model.

The thought of those arthritic feet in spiked heels curled Mr. Morton's lips into a smirk. His eighth graders would have had a field day.

The smirk was blossoming into a chuckle, but it died when he saw the second mannequin. A cowboy. From the weathered hat to the muddy boots, the mannequin looked fresh from the ranch. The sight shriveled whatever was left of Mr. Morton's insides.

Why?

A flash, a pop, and he was back.

Back where?

His sedan, in the left-turn lane rolling up to a red light, and luck was with him. First in line, he'd get the green arrow and avoid the stress of navigating oncoming traffic while the drivers behind grew impatient. It was Christmas Eve, and he could feel the tension building.

Martha, in the passenger seat, was debating her decision to wear a maroon dress. Velvet? What had she been thinking? They were spending Christmas Eve at Gwen's house, not the White House. They needed to go back so she could change. They shouldn't be going at all, barging in on Gwen and Andy with Gwen days away from giving birth. What was wrong with them?

Mr. Morton heard honking. Had he spaced the green arrow?

He looked up from the offending maroon dress into the grill of a beat-up blue pickup. The pickup had veered into the intersection. It was barreling straight at the Mortons' sedan.

The truck was being driven by a cowboy hat. Not an angry face or a drunk face. A cowboy hat slumped forward so Mr. Morton could see the brim all the way around.

He threw a protective arm across Martha's chest. It was all he had time to do. The last thing he remembered was that cowboy hat smashing through the windshield like a cannonball.

Mr. Morton was sitting on the department store floor, legs splayed like chicken wings, bare butt on prickly midnight-blue carpet. He didn't remember how he got there.

The elderly retail thief was long gone.

He was alone with the cowboy and the now barefooted bombshell.

And he was dead.

Where was Martha? Had the passed-out cowboy killed her too?

Please, no. Not with Gwen days from becoming a new mom. The world thought Gwen was all grown-up, but Mr. Morton knew better. Gwen was a dreamy-eyed little girl with curly brown pigtails and a handful of pretty shells in her pocket.

Gwen needed her mom. Andy was as new to parenting as Gwen, and he was a math professor. New dads—especially scientific ones—were no replacement for a grandma.

Using the display case, Mr. Morton pushed himself back to his feet and scanned the heads nearby for a dyed-black hairdo. One that had been aiming for Elizabeth Taylor but landed somewhere nearer Edward Scissorhands. A scaredo, his eighth graders would have called it.

Martha. The love of his life. The mother of his child. If she was here, he had to find her.

He wandered barefoot between empty racks, passing mannequins dressed as everything from scientists to strippers. Some wore shoes. Some didn't.

The overhead lights burned sunlight white. In the unforgiving glow, every blemish should have stood out like spilt red wine. But the people he passed had no blemishes. Everyone's skin, though as wrinkly as his, was wiped clean. No scars. No moles. Not so much as a freckle.

Some people looked even more lost than he did. Others had made themselves right at home, strutting about in diamonds and rubies pilfered from mannequins. But not even they were wearing shoes. To the last person, everyone was barefoot.

As far as Mr. Morton wandered, he never spotted a cashier. Eventually, though, he stumbled upon the elevator bank. Cableless glass elevators came and went as quiet as jellyfish.

Leaning over a polished gold railing, Mr. Morton looked up and down the elevator shaft. The effect was as disorienting as a carnival funhouse. The floors seemed to go on and on in both directions forever, like the department store never ended.

A white-neon sign overhead told him he was on the seventy-second floor. Below the neon sign, another sign was attracting attention. This sign, a scroll tall as the passing elevators, glittered with gold-leaf script and hovered like a paper hummingbird. Around it, a jostling crowd of bedsheets jockeyed for a closer look.

Mr. Morton joined the crowd. He considered asking the woman to his right what the fuss was about, but she kept using an index finger to press glasses that were no longer there up the bridge of her nose. He decided to wait his turn.

When he reached the front of the crush, the beautiful scroll was a bit of a letdown. The golden script was tiny and hard to read. He stared at it, but the letters wouldn't form words. Then he realized they weren't in English.

He looked the sign up and down. It was the same message repeated in hundreds of languages. Every language on Earth, he guessed.

Despite complaints from behind that needed no translation, Mr. Morton took the time he needed to find the English version and read it through twice.

Welcome to the Department Store. Browse as long as you like.

When you find the outfit you want to wear in your next life, please take the shoes to the checkout counter on the first floor.*

As his companions wandered away, Mr. Morton dropped his gaze to the asterisk.

*Due to increased demand, the Department Store can no longer guarantee an eternal shopping experience. To avoid random selection, it's recommended that you limit your browsing to twelve hours. Management apologizes for any inconvenience.

Pinballing out of the crowd, Mr. Morton beelined for the gold railing. Gripped it. He wasn't sure if he breathed anymore, but he needed fresh air.

Twelve hours to find Martha, and he had already wasted so much time. Why did it always take him so long to process things? Maybe for his next life he would choose to be a mathematician like Andy instead of a failed writer turned eighth-grade reading teacher.

Martha. Where would she be?

Mr. Morton looked at the neon sign. Seventy-two. That number was familiar. Why? He searched back through his memories to his last birthday cake. Two candles. Seven. Two. He took another look at the crowd. Every face was as wrinkled as his.

The next elevator that arrived, Mr. Morton stepped on and pressed a glowing opal button etched with the number sixty-seven. If Martha was here, that's where he'd find her.

The sixty-seventh floor looked like the seventy-second. Same layout. Same lighting. Same assortment of mannequins. The people were the same too but younger, their wrinkles grouped in tight cliques around their eyes and lips.

Mr. Morton searched around the elevator bank first. Many of the women looked like Martha, but none had Martha's scaredo.

As he worked his way through the stacks, he noticed a pattern in people's rope belts. Some were gold like his. Others bronze. Others dingy brown. The more at home the person looked, the more faded their rope. It was the plain brown ropes who wore pilfered jewelry.

He was getting a feel for the layout of the department store too. The mannequins nearest the elevators promised riches and adventure—rockstars and astronauts, models and movie stars, moguls and financiers. Most of the shoes on those mannequins were long gone.

The farther back into the stacks you went, the humbler the shopping experience. There, the mannequins wore the working clothes of farmers and school teachers, bus drivers and construction workers, and, for the most part, they still wore their sensible flats and work boots.

Mr. Morton was confused. He had seen Earth. Walked its streets. Even the biggest cities didn't reflect the shoes that were disappearing. If the missing shoes forecast Earth's population, most everyone would be in politics or jet-setting to their next movie premier.

Between the department store and Earth, something was getting lost in translation.

Regardless, the more Mr. Morton looked, the lighter he felt. Martha wasn't here. She had survived. The new baby would have a grandma.

Around the time he reached the mannequins dressed like prison guards and meatpackers, he discovered his rope had begun to tarnish bronze. Time was running low already.

He picked up his pace. Tried asking people he passed if they had seen a woman with a beautiful smile and an unfortunate hairdo. No one had. No one seemed interested.

At some point, Mr. Morton's search brought him to a wall. The edge of the department store. The bounds of the afterlife. The wall had no windows. No way to look out and see where the department store was. Just more empty shelves.

Curious, he followed the wall. Though he never found a corner, he found a counter and a long line of people waiting at it.

A neon sign above the counter read, "Layaway."

Below the neon sign, a floating scroll.

Mr. Morton scanned the gold-leaf script till he found English.

Can't find the life you're looking for? Don't worry! Layaway until the life you want becomes available. For a deposit of three years off your new life and installments of one additional year per week of layaway, you can buy the life of your dreams.

The line stretched past the mannequins dressed for the dirtiest jobs and into the trade jobs and desk work. Everyone in line held a trinket from a mannequin. Luxury items. Diamond necklaces. Designer bags. Oversized sunglasses.

Mr. Morton walked the line. As he did, another kind of luxury caught his eye. Not the glimmer of real gems but the sheen of fake velvet. Polyester pomp.

A mannequin off to the right was wearing a cheap velvet dress. Maroon. The outfit was unwanted, its shoes untouched. But that was because people didn't know better. The woman who chose those shoes would have a happy life. Quiet, but happy.

Mr. Morton grabbed up a handful of fabric. Crushed it in his fist.

Martha was here.

He wanted to tear the dress from the mannequin and hug it to himself.

Something bounced against the velvet.

Something on a string.

A tag.

Mr. Morton grabbed up the tag. Read.

Housewife
One husband. One child.

Health: 8
Wealth: 3
Talent: 3
Happiness: 5
Longevity: 7

Happiness: 5? Five out of what? Ten? Surely not.

Mr. Morton read the tag again. And again.

Five.

A typo. It had to be. The tag was wrong. Or the outfit was. This wasn't Martha's dress at all. The mannequins wore representative outfits, not the clothes a person died in. This dress was off-the-rack. There must have been hundreds made. Thousands. This was someone else's.

He'd prove it.

Dashing past the construction workers and telemarketers and back through the socialites and influencers, Mr. Morton leapt onto the first empty elevator and punched the opal etched with seventy-two.

The elevator door whooshed closed. Mr. Morton glanced down at his rope as the last of the gold flecked away. His rope was completely bronze.

No. Not yet. He had to prove Martha wasn't here. That wasn't her outfit. Her happiness wasn't a five. It couldn't be. They were happy together.

On floor seventy-two, Mr. Morton raced past the rich mannequins. He didn't know exactly where his own outfit would be, but he had an idea. Somewhere past the lawyers and doctors and bankers. Past the nurses and professors and writers.

When polyester replaced silk, Mr. Morton slowed down. He was getting close. Half-walking, half-jogging, he hurried from platform to platform. Uniforms. Costume jewelry. Knockoff shoes. None of the trinkets were missing. None of the shoes were gone. The only people wandering these aisles wore shiny new ropes.

On and on. And then, there it was—his mannequin. Plaid

sweater. Pleated chinos. Faded penny loafers. Not the outfit he died in, but close enough. It was the uniform of his life. At first, Martha had bought him other kinds of clothes—jeans, polos, button-up shirts. But he had always gravitated back to plaid sweaters and chinos, and she had finally relented.

He made his way through the empty racks to his mannequin, and there, at its feet, sat a woman whose dyed-black hairdo just missed Elizabeth Taylor.

Mr. Morton stopped and soaked up the beautiful features of his wife's face.

Of course, she was here. She had always been the quick one in the family.

He wanted to say her name, but the words that came out were, "Ms. Hildegard."

Not Martha.

Not even Mrs. Morton.

Ms. Hildegard.

As if she had never taken his name.

As if he hadn't spent a lifetime loving her.

Mr. Morton wanted to scoop her up. Instead, he waited for her to say something.

What she finally said was so Martha it brought tears to his eyes.

With the little smirk he knew so well, she said, "I thought I'd find you here."

He wanted to say something romantic, but the words that tumbled out were decidedly not. "The cowboy killed us. Gwen's having a baby, and the cowboy killed us."

Ms. Hildegard shrugged. She was hugging a pair of boots to her chest. Heavy boots. Black with a shocking yellow stripe. Mud caked thick in the chunky treads.

"What," Mr. Morton hesitated. "What are those?"

Ms. Hildegard gazed down at the boots as if at her first grand-child. A look of such unbounded love that it made Mr. Morton's knees buckle.

She held up the boots for Mr. Morton's inspection. "Mountaineering boots. Me mountaineering. Can you imagine?"

Mr. Morton tried to sound casual. "Not really. You don't like hiking."

Ms. Hildegard smiled. "That was the old me. The new me loves hiking. I'm going to summit peaks. Denali. Kilimanjaro. Everest. I'm going to see the world."

Mr. Morton swallowed. "But what about Gwen and the new baby? Aren't you worried?"

Ms. Hildegard frowned. "Gwen will be fine. She's all grown up. And she has Andy."

"But we'll never meet our grandbaby. We'll miss his first words, his first steps."

Ms. Hildegard shook her head. "You mustn't think about it like that. That life is done. We gave Gwen everything she needs to succeed. We gave her everything we had. She'll be fine."

Mr. Morton stumbled over his words. Stopped. Tried again. "Our grandbaby is here right now. Somewhere in this store. What color is his rope? Bronze? Brown? Does it matter? Whatever shoes he picks, it's not what he'll become. Something's wrong with this place."

Ms. Hildegard waved Mr. Morton's fears away. "You always were so literal. The shoes don't guarantee the outcome. They nudge you is all. It's up to you to make it happen. The baby will make it happen. So will I. This time, I'm going to follow my dreams. You should too."

Mr. Morton gulped. "I did follow my dreams. I had you and Gwen. It was everything I wanted."

The smirk was back. "That's a lie and you know it. You wanted to be a writer. You used to shut us out, me and Gwen. Tell us to leave you alone. You were writing your novel."

Mr. Morton remembered. He had yearned to see his name in print. Why?

"I was wrong. Publishing didn't matter. Nothing matters but

you and Gwen and the baby. We have to find our way back to them."

"No." The word was short. Final. Martha would never have spoken to him that way.

"But—"

"No. That life is over. The sooner you accept it, the happier your next life will be."

"But we at least have to find a way to be together. We're partners."

Ms. Hildegard's features softened. She stood and caressed Mr. Morton's cheek.

"I cherish the life we shared. But I want adventure this time. I want my lungs to burn from lack of oxygen."

"I'll come with you."

"No. I want to push myself to the limit. I can't ask you to join me."

"You don't have to ask. I'll go find some mountaineering boots right now."

Mr. Morton turned, but Ms. Hildegard grabbed his arm and patted it as if soothing a puppy.

"No. This is my journey, not yours. I want to do it on my own."

Mr. Morton wanted to protest. Wanted to tear the boots from her hands and throw them down the elevator shaft. He sighed. It was Gwen announcing her engagement all over again. "Can I come with you to checkout?"

Ms. Hildegard smiled, nodded.

The elevator ride to the first floor was like a flipbook in reverse. Floor by floor, the years dropped away. First the wrinkles disappeared. Then the weariness. The fifties. Forties. Thirties. With each floor, Mr. Morton remembered his own life backward. Acceptance, disappointment, disillusionment, fear, confidence, excitement.

Excitement. He remembered it now. How it felt to be twenty.

The giddiness of being alive. Of being at the start. Heart light with promise.

Descending through the twenties tore Mr. Morton apart, but the teens put him back together again. The cacophony of youth. Belligerent faces and torn bedsheets. Mannequins rearranged. Empty hangers twisted into monuments of teenage rage millennia in the making.

Then, like a salve, the teens gave way to preteens, and finally, most precious of all, childhood. Pudgy little feet meant to be barefoot. A few children sprawled, weeping and wiping runny noses on smudged bedsheets, but most skipped and laughed and climbed the empty shelves as nimbly as they would monkey bars.

On the lowest floors, the shelves and racks teemed with babies. Cooing. Crying. Crawling. No mannequins at all. Nothing to do but wait.

Then, everything went dark. For a moment that lasted an eternity, everything was gone. Ms. Hildegard, the elevator, the universe. Mr. Morton was alone. Then, the light returned, and the elevator stopped. They had reached the ground floor.

The ground floor was a great hall, tall and echoey as a train station, paneled in varnished wood. On one side, benches lined the wall. On the other, automated checkout stands beeped and purred. In between, crowds milled about, bidding each other farewell.

A floating scroll gave gold-leaf instructions, but the process was simple. You donned your chosen shoes and walked to a checkout stand. The automated checkout printed you a ticket. You took the ticket to a pair of pearl-encrusted gates and inserted the ticket into the slot. The pearly gates opened, and you stepped through. That was it. No returns. No exchanges.

Ms. Hildegard didn't hesitate. She sat down and slipped the big mountaineering boots onto her tiny feet. When she stood up again, she seemed taller.

She didn't hug Mr. Morton goodbye, but she caressed his

cheek. A second later, with a beep and a whoosh, the pearly gates opened, and Ms. Hildegard was gone. She didn't look back.

When the gates clicked closed again, it was like they snapped Mr. Morton's heart in two. Something inside him cracked. He heard it over the din. It was real. He looked down to see if he was bleeding. He wasn't, but his rope had begun to decay again. It was turning brown.

His bare feet were shuffling backward before he realized. When his brain caught up, he turned and sprinted for the elevator.

The arriving elevators were crowded with footwear from flippers to ballet slippers. Mr. Morton bounced from one bare foot to the other, impatient.

When an elevator finally emptied, he scrambled on and punched the opal etched seventy-two. The elevator lifted. Darkness. Babies. Toddlers. Life in order. Mr. Morton couldn't watch it. Not again. He closed his eyes.

When the elevator stopped, Mr. Morton blinked his eyes open and saw wrinkles. Relief flooded him. His own floor. He checked the neon sign. Sure enough. Seventy-two.

He darted off the elevator and ran. Past the expensive suits and tailored shirts. Past the bangles and glitter. He dodged empty shelves and empty racks. He weaved around wandering bedsheets. His feet knew where they were going. Knew where they wanted to be.

He found it without effort. His own outfit. His own shoes.

Scrambling with shaking fingers, he found his tag.

Eighth grade reading teacher
One wife. One child.
Health: 7
Wealth: 3
Talent: 4
Happiness: 9
Longevity: 7

Happiness nine.

Nine.

How could his be nine when Martha's was only five? When he was only a failed writer?

Mr. Morton read the tag again.

It didn't say failed writer.

Not anywhere.

He flipped it over to be sure.

No. He was an eighth grade reading teacher. And he was happy.

He knew it.

On the back, Mr. Morton found a disclaimer in curly gold script. He had to hold the tag up to the light to read it.

Return Policy: If you select your own shoes, proceed to Returns on the top floor.

Mr. Morton squeezed the plaid sweater his mannequin wore— a gift from Martha from a time when he believed her happiness equaled his own. He loved that sweater.

Returns.

That's what he wanted. It's what he had wanted from the moment he arrived.

But he had to move fast. His rope was mostly brown. His time was nearly up. He could be snatched away any second, deposited into a life he didn't want.

Mr. Morton snatched one penny loafer then the other. Hugging the familiar footwear to his chest, he ran for the elevator.

It took him an eon to catch an elevator. Every elevator already had people on it, and all the people were going down. Down to younger floors. Down to the ground floor. Down.

Finally, an empty elevator arrived. He darted on and punched the highest opal of all. The bedsheets who had followed him on wrinkled their noses and shuffled off again.

The glass door closed, and Mr. Morton whisked away.

Outside the glass, the department store remained the same,

but the faces changed. Not much at first and then all at once. The faces turned old. So old. Mr. Morton closed his eyes.

At the chime, the glass door slid open.

Mr. Morton opened his eyes. The light was blinding white. He blinked and tried to shield his eyes with his hand, but the light came from everywhere.

Hugging his penny loafers closer, Mr. Morton inched off the elevator and waited for his eyes to adjust. Behind him, the elevator chimed and dropped away.

Squinting, Mr. Morton looked around. The layout was familiar, similar to the lower floors. But here, there were no mannequins. No people at all.

And the shelves were stocked. The racks too. On the golden hangers draped bedsheets and ropes. And the shelves held rows of shoes. Shoes of every shape and size. A few were fine. Most were like his own. Old. Worn. Well-loved.

Beyond the racks, far in the back, a sign was just visible. The room was bright but the sign brighter still. It was the brightest light Mr. Morton had ever seen. Returns.

Mr. Morton found an empty space between a pair of worn-out sneakers and a pair of faded slippers. After one last hug, he deposited the penny loafers on the shelf.

He untied his rope. Only a glimmer or two of bronze remained. His time was up.

Pulling the bedsheet over his head, he hung it on an empty hanger, draped the rope around the hanger's neck, and deposited his hanger back on the rack by the others.

For a brief moment in the buff, he wondered how many lives he had lived.

Then, he walked toward Returns.

———

A couple sat side-by-side under a Christmas tree decorated with homemade ornaments. The man wore a brand-new plaid sweater. The woman, very pregnant, wore tears on both cheeks.

"How can they be gone?" The woman hugged her swollen belly. "I can't do this without them. I don't even want to."

The man wrapped his arms around her. Pulled her close. "It'll be okay, Gwen. We have each other. We have everything your parents taught us. We can do this."

She sobbed.

He pressed his cheek to her soft hair. As he did, he glimpsed an unopened package under the tree, buried beneath crumpled wrapping paper, a plain brown package.

The man sat up, forcing his wife up too.

Sniffling, the woman followed his gaze. When her eyes landed on the package, her head tilted. "What's that?"

"Don't know."

The woman wiped her eyes, leaned under the boughs, and pulled the package out. It was small enough to fit in the palm of her hand, tied with twine.

The twine glinted in the light. The woman held the package up to the Christmas tree. Sure enough, the twine had a hint, just a speckle or two, of bronze.

The couple looked at each other.

"Did you put it there?" asked one.

"No." An emphatic shake of the head. "You?"

The couple looked at the gift.

The woman pulled the twine. The bow unraveled and the bronze crumbled away.

Hands shaking, the woman ripped the brown paper back to reveal a white box.

Inside was a pair of baby shoes, brown leather with a tiny tassel on the toes.

The woman jumped like she had been slapped.

The husband caught her. "What's wrong?"

The woman sniffled and smiled a little.

Lifting the penny loafers to her nose, she breathed in. Deep and long.

"Can't you smell that?"

The husband sniffed. "No. What?"

The woman breathed in again.

"These shoes smell just like my father. It's like he's here with us."

The woman hugged the baby shoes to her chest, and the man hugged his wife to him. Both watched the Christmas tree twinkle and waited for the baby to kick.

GRANDMA AND THE VIRGINIA TECH MURDERER

OLIVE WOOLLEY BURT AWARDS, FIRST PLACE, GENERAL CREATIVE NONFICTION

LAUREL YEATES

My grandmother cried. I kept my head down, playing with a toy on the floor of my grandparents' living room. *My living room.* In this 67-year-old memory, I'm feigning disinterest in what was happening around me. My mother and my great aunt sat, legs crossed at the knees, on a turquoise sectional sofa, my great aunt smoking in a frantic puff-puff-puff sort of way. My grandfather paced around the room, worn hardwood creaking in predictable places. He wrung his hands. My aunt, just fourteen, sat wide-eyed, clearly troubled, knees bouncing. My grandmother pleaded to be allowed to stay at home. She didn't want to go away again. My mother and grandfather, in their heartache and sanity, tried to reassure her. She will come home soon, they said. We will all go visit her, they said. It has to be done, they said. I kept my head down. I don't remember the toy.

On April 16, 2007, 23-year-old Cho Seung-Hui, a senior at Virginia Polytechnic Institute, barricaded himself in Virginia Tech's Norris Hall, where he used two semi-automatic hand pistols to kill thirty-two people and injure seventeen, finally turning the gun on himself as police breached his barricade. This event breathed unwanted life into memories of my grandmother's schizophrenia.

It was twenty-four years since her death. Since then, much has changed with major strides being made in the treatment for this disorder and others like it. Finally, new research shows some promise of figuring out the genesis of this particular disease that cuts such a mighty swath of pain through the lives of its chosen families.

Public perception of the mentally ill has unquestionably improved, at least enough that the horror of asylums, so painfully exposed in the 1950s, has been replaced by more compassionate, humane clinical settings and facilities that serve and shelter the mentally fragile. That kind of mistreatment and neglect will not be tolerated again.

But are mistreatment and neglect just wearing new faces? In this third decade of a new century, mental illness is much more in our faces than it has ever been. If we don't know someone who is certifiably mentally ill, we undoubtedly know or know about someone in our social circle who has sought treatment through counseling or medication for emotional or mental disorders. In the more extreme manifestations, we are now all too familiar with the face and behavior of untreated—or poorly treated—mental illness as seen in many of the faces of the homeless who live on our streets.

Finding myself in the path of one of these people, I can't help but think about the worst-case scenario. What if he or she is dangerous? If approached, how tolerant should I be? When I act, will it be out of a true gut instinct or out of the knowledge formed from my earliest memories about how distorted life can be for these unfortunate victims?

On a cool summer day—unusual for Salt Lake City in July—I passed over my usual sunsuit in favor of a green plaid dress with a broad white collar, designed and sewn by my own grandmother. My grandmother and I were going to town. We would catch the bus at the corner for the ten-minute ride to the south side of Temple Square, where we would shop first at ZCMI, the preeminent department store in this hub of Mormons, the first to open under the leadership of the famous Mormon leader, Brigham Young. On this day we were looking for fabric for a swim bag for my first swimming lessons.

On our way to the bus, my grandmother and I held hands. I skipped and talked. Just five years old, I was a chatty child with much to say, many observations needing to be spoken, and a precocious desire to fill quiet spaces. At the bus stop, my grandmother reached into her purse for the clear plastic cosmetic bag that held her change. She pressed a coin into my hand, along with a mint "pill," as I called them, one of the chalky mints that were her signature candy of choice. Sometimes she had pink ones. Today, they were white.

On the bus, we sat in the first pair of seats that faced forward on the driver's side. The bus was quiet; just a few solitary passengers riding to town in the late morning. With hands folded in my lap, I stopped the chatter and moved the mint from side to side in my mouth. My grandmother stared straight ahead. She sighed deeply, and when I looked up at her, I saw a furrowed brow and pursed angry lips. My hand reached out for hers. She received it, squeezed it, then let it go.

Her chatter began, at first as a whisper. A whisper through clenched teeth. "Don't you dare come near them. You don't even know me. You're not welcome here. Get away from us." I reached across my body and lightly touched her forearm. "It's all right, Grammy," I whispered. Her face relaxed, the tension in her hands dissipating. For a moment. And then it built again.

The bus pulled away from a stop and two women paid then looked for seats nearby. My grandmother, staring at nothing—or something?— said through clenched teeth, "You are nothing but filth. The scum of the earth." She clenched then relaxed her fists. "You are the perpetrators of all that is bad. Get away from my children, and you get away from me." The two women hurried to seats near the back of the bus. Rubbing her arm, I whispered to my grandma, "It's okay, Grammy. We're almost to town."

That day, the demons were left on the bus. We walked through the children's section of ZCMI, my grandmother making mental notes and *gathering ideas for dresses she would make for my cousin Alice and me. We stopped at a small café; she counted out change from the plastic cosmetic purse to pay for two limeades. At a table, she produced a piece of scrap paper with a pleasing drawing of a duck—a blueprint for the swim bag she planned to make. Within days, a goldish-brown striped sale remnant was transformed—with the help of rickrack, embroidery, and appliqués—into a duck with an opening along its back and a handle at the top of its head. Wings, attached on either side, held a quilted parasol and a quilted bucket. Alice got one, too. Treasures from our magical grandmother.*

That Cho's roommates and fellow students had concerns about Cho's unusual behavior may serve as a red flag we would all like to believe demands definitive action. Yet, many of us can recount examples of inappropriate and puzzling scenarios related to people we have known who never just wake up one day and kill thirty-three people including themselves. We can speculate about the shooter's motivation, preparedness, and opportunity, but the reality is that, for reasons unknown, all the stars were aligned at that moment for that madness to happen.

Could things have been different? If Cho was on regular medication, maybe he had skipped it for a few days. Perhaps an unexpected call from his mother might have distracted and diverted him from the drastic actions that made him famous. A cold or an upset stomach might have bought him some time before sealing his fate and the fate of forty-nine other victims, along with drastically affecting the countless family members and friends of those victims and the entire university community.

For my grandmother, her position as a stay-at-home wife and mother in a very traditional Mormon community in the mid-20th century assured that she was surrounded by protection, a protection Cho's family could not maintain. After all, he was an ostensibly bright young man who seemed to function—if only marginally well—on his own.

Maybe it was a cultural issue that inhibited appropriate action by Cho's family members: Koreans seeking assimilation into American culture. Maybe it was a lack of education or understanding. Perhaps it was a wrong or misunderstood diagnosis or inconsistent medical intervention for a young man living away from home on a college campus.

In my grandmother's case, her culture and the era of her illness facilitated her protection. Operating as much out of shame and ignorance as survival or compassion, my family circled the wagons and made sure my grandmother was away from those who might be frightened by her behavior or misunderstand her condition. We surrounded her with our love and vigilance. Over and over, our presence, and often our physical contact, brought a touch of reality to her.

Two police officers appeared at the door. My great aunt was the first to speak with them. A phone call had been made to the state capitol, and the caller—someone at this address—had spoken to someone in the attorney general's office. The attorney general's life had been threatened.

It was one of two times my grandmother was involuntarily committed to the state hospital in Orem. She went "voluntarily" at least six other times. Her visits usually lasted four to eight weeks. During those weeks, her doctors would use some of the new drugs on her, experimenting with various dosages. She participated daily in group therapy sessions and on at least two occasions received electric shock therapy.

When she came home, she was consistently the mild-mannered, sweet, and loving woman we all knew her to be when her demons were not hounding her. In fact, her pleasing demeanor was so consistent and unwavering that there was no question it was the result of the drug regimen concocted for her during her most recent hospitalization.

Following her commitment for the threat on the attorney general's life, two of her sisters and their very best friends planned a meeting of "Club." Club was a monthly gathering of a dozen or so middle-aged women who had known each other since their youth. They either planned a special lunch or dinner at the home of one of the Club members or they went to a special restaurant. In celebration of my grandmother's return from the hospital, they chose a lunch at The Hawaiian, a trendy new restaurant that served Chinese food in surroundings reminiscent of tiki huts. Every twenty minutes, to the delight of the diners, a crack of thunder would signal the oncoming "storm" of lightning and more thunder, with rain falling around the perimeter of the central dining area.

Having Club at The Hawaiian was a dressing up occasion. My grandmother, who stood 5 feet, 10 inches tall in bare feet, knew how to dress. In expensive gray wool she had purchased from a sale table and fashioned into a stylish sheath, she accessorized with earrings and a scarf of sea blue that reflected the amazing blue of her eyes. So often, those eyes looked startled and disturbed, but today, they were sparkly and kind.

In the restaurant, as Club members were shown to their table, they passed the attorney general having lunch with his wife. About to sit down, a spark of recognition led my grandmother to retrace her steps to the couple's table. By the time my great-aunts realized what had drawn my grandmother back, they approached her to hear her say to the attorney general, "Excuse me, they tell me that I called you and threatened your life. Can you imagine that? I don't believe that was me, but if it was, I am so sorry."

The attorney general, looking stricken and alarmed, nodded to my two aunts in acknowledgment and gratitude as they each linked an arm through my grandmother's arms and led her back to the Club table.

In the days following the VT shooting, the various media outlets harped on what happened, why it happened, and what could have been done differently to keep it from happening again. First, there probably should be prohibitions preventing the effortless purchase of guns by people identified by professionals as unstable, but there weren't any. Professors did intervene and take actions they thought might help him. But it wasn't enough. Administrators might have responded to expressed concerns with more definitive actions. Now, it's unlikely they will ever minimize red flags such as these if they are ever faced with them again.

But, with Cho's sullen, unsmiling face splashed across the television screen twenty-four hours each day, I thought back to that question about mistreatment and neglect. Cho's family and community failed him in the same way a person with any other kind of disability would have been cheated if left to navigate this difficult life with little support or attention. The mistreatment came in the form not of abuse but of *improper* treatment. That neglect left him open to actions he couldn't control or understand. And in the end, he was mistreated once more by his vilification in front of the world.

Undoubtedly, the Cho family grieves with the world over the randomness and the horrific loss from this event. But now, they also get to second guess themselves for the rest of their lives and carry the guilt of not doing more than they did. I think of the sweet baby Cho must have been, a joy to his parents and big sister. He had an obvious level of functionality as evidenced by his near completion of a four-year degree from a respected university. His sister, a bright and successful young woman, expressed her love for him as well as their family's observances that he just seemed "quiet." If they didn't realize how much this young man's illness impacted their lives before the shooting, they do now.

There was no one to play with. The August sun was high and hot, and truth be told, it felt better to be in the cool of the back bedroom of the house. Grandma was resting as she did during the day, a chance to make up for her sleepless nights, lying on her back next to my grandpa, staring at the ceiling, vigilant in the dark, protecting her family from the evil she knew was lying in wait for an opportunity to move in. She drank coffee through the night, sometimes several pots, getting up many times for a fresh cup, then walking silently through the other bedrooms, checking on her loved ones. By morning, as we all started our daily routines, she would turn onto her side, ready for a few hours of sleep.

On this day, she slept most of the morning. Sitting on the floor at the foot of her bed, I had spent my day's early hours transforming two cardboard boxes into a doll house. One box, on its side, formed the frame, and the other, cut up into pieces, made up the walls and the furniture. I used my uncle's lined binder paper to make a paper doll family, which I colored with three crayons I found in the corner junk cupboard.

Grandma stirred; I waited, hardly able to contain my excitement about showing her what I had made. She rose to sit on the side of the bed, greeting me by my nickname. "Hi, Laurie," she said with aching tenderness. Careful to not jump the gun and hit her with my creation before she was ready, I waited until she got her fresh morning—late morning—coffee then came back to lie on the bed, first propping up all of the pillows so that she could sit up to receive the world.

"Grandma, do you want to see what I made?" She smoothed the bedclothes on Grandpa's side of the bed and said lovingly, "Of course." As I showed her the house and its accoutrements, she carefully handled each piece, admiring my handiwork. "Have you made up their story yet?" she asked. I shook my head but then launched into a scenario that seemed to please my grandmother. As she listened, she stared at the wall just past the foot of the bed, a half-smile on her face. With the story finished, I retreated into the mumbling prattle of a six-year-old child engaged in play, almost silently acting out the daily lives of my paper family.

In the corner of my eye, I saw my grandmother's right hand take a familiar shape: her fingers were brought tightly together in a cup shape, her thumb drawn into the recess of the cup. There was tension in this posture; it was an affectation she used to make her point as she admonished her demons. Her brow was furrowed. She spoke softly, too softly for me to hear her actual words, but I knew what she was saying. She was calling someone "the scum of the earth," "too filthy for this life." The unknown entity to whom she spoke was dispatched, as it would be repeatedly throughout the day. Occasionally, she flattened her hand and slapped the bed at her side. A soft whisper from me or a question to bring her back to my world calmed the wave of delusion for a time. Then, it returned.

. . .

The workings of my life have improved, thanks to years of self-reflection, information gathering, a degree in psychology, and various therapies. I know now that the seeds of codependence were planted on the day I was born into that household and that as I grew and learned to not rock the boat for fear of adding to the chaos, that dysfunction took root with a fierceness that took years to uproot and heal.

At a very young age, I learned that some people, older and seemingly more powerful than I, were much more fragile and needed protecting. I learned to subvert my childish needs and concerns as there were much bigger needs within my household. I became a caretaker when I should have been taken care of myself.

But I also learned how much joy I brought to a woman who lived her life with immense, paralyzing fear. Sometimes, she spent her last few coins before the end of the month on animal crackers for me to frost with icing she made in four different colors. She set up tea parties with finger sandwiches and milk poured into little shot glasses she called elf dishes. She mixed chocolate milk in Kerr canning jars then added raisins wrapped in paper napkins and sandwiches made with butter and sugar on white bread to a big paper bag for me to take outside into the backyard where I hosted picnics for my neighborhood playmates.

When confronted with the graphic footage and recounted tales of horror that Cho perpetrated at Virginia Tech, I hoped that some people might see beyond that. Imbedded in that walking time bomb, somewhere there must have been some goodness. I believe it was there because during every single day of my childhood and for years into my young adulthood, my grandmother taught me about courage, acceptance, patience, devotion and the true goodness of people that can sometimes be obscured by ignorance and misunderstanding.

THE HAM SANDWICH

OLIVE WOOLLEY BURT AWARDS, SECOND PLACE, GENERAL & LITERARY FICTION
LINDA F. SMITH

y client, a down-on-his-luck homeless guy, had been picked up for shoplifting from—where else—Walmart." I began one of my intended-to-be inspirational talks to the half-dozen legal defenders I was charged with mentoring. Most of them had begun this career with dreams of becoming Atticus Finch and had since become something between frustrated and disillusioned. They'd already faced cynical prosecutors, bureaucratic judges, and ungrateful clients. It was my job to give them a reason to carry on. "I was young, like you, and naïve, when this client taught me the most important lesson of my career." They looked up from brown bag lunches, giving me grudging permission to try to convince them justice existed.

I continued to set the stage. Walmart on 1300 South had stationed a permanent police officer where they made more arrests than any other place in the county, mostly due to the fact that the poor shopped there.

I met my client, "Jim," at his first hearing in Justice Court, when the judge would tell the defendant what the charges were, ask if he needed to have counsel appointed for him, and set bail. I didn't need to describe the bland courtroom to them, as it had not changed over the years. They could picture the beige walls and green linoleum tiles, the massive oaken doors, the messy tables counsel occupied, and the raised bench from which the judge presided. The rules provided that the defendant should not be asked to enter a plea until he had a chance to confer with counsel, but regularly the prosecutors pressured us to present their deals to our clients to clear the docket, and just as regularly judges accepted the guilty pleas, rushed though they were.

The clerk called out Jim's name, but I didn't pay any notice until I heard him asserting himself loudly, "Yes, I do want an attorney." The judge motioned for me to approach, and the city attorney handed me the paperwork for the case—charging documents, police report, and rap sheet. I entered my appearance in the case and asked the court to grant me a short recess to confer with my client. I introduced myself to Jim, a middle-aged man with long greying hair, a bushy beard, and rumpled mismatched clothing, and we moseyed out to the hall.

I began to read the file even as Jim pressed me about his case. The charges were "retail theft," and the police report indicated "store security officer observed suspect place sandwich in his coat pocket" and "suspect passed cashier without paying for item" and "security officer stopped suspect before he exited store."

Jim interrupted my perusal. "The security guard was so out of line. Pushed me, grabbed my arm, near pulled it out of the socket." Jim waggled his left arm at me, perhaps trying to demonstrate it was even now dislocated. "Still hurts, yow, yessir." I nodded to let Jim continue. "They don't got a case anyhow—I never even left the store. Just a five-dollar ham-and-cheese sandwich. Anyhow."

I nodded before addressing Jim. "It says here that you put a sandwich in your pocket and walked past the cashier. Is that what happened? Will the store cameras show that?"

"Yeah, but it's bogus."

"In what way? What do you mean, bogus?"

"It was just a sandwich, bro. I hadn't eaten all day."

I nodded again and asked if Jim would excuse me for a

minute. I went back inside the courtroom to find the prosecutor. "What's the offer on this case?" I asked. "It was only a sandwich, and this guy's record is all just piddling stuff like this."

The prosecutor, a burly man at least twenty years my senior, buttoned and unbuttoned the suit coat stretched tight around his middle and checked his notes. "Plead guilty to one count of retail theft, no jail time, standard fine and costs."

I rolled my eyes. "So, this homeless guy is going to pay around $500 for trying to get something to eat?"

"That's the standard offer. What do you want me to do?" the prosecutor responded.

"Dismiss the charges. Use your prosecutorial discretion—be a minister of justice and just let this one go."

He laughed, "How old are you buddy? Please communicate the offer to your client, counsel."

Bruce, one of my mentees, reacted. "What an a-hole!"

Yes, I affirmed—a.k.a. a governmental bureaucrat just "doing his job."

In the courthouse, I returned to Jim who had been waiting in the hall. Other attorneys conferred with their clients up and down the wide hallway, and family groups whispered together as they waited for their attorneys to find them. Jim listened to the offer then shook his head. "No way I can pay all that. And I've already got fifty more hours of community service for a bogus trespassing case from last year. No deal."

I did my best to try to convince Jim that a guilty plea at this point was his best option. First, there was no defense. Walking past the cashiers with a sandwich hidden in his pocket is all they had to show to prove intent to steal. Walmart had cameras all over; they would probably have film of him taking the sandwich and putting it in his pocket. They would certainly have film that showed him walking past the cashiers. Second, if we entered a not-guilty plea and scheduled the case for a pre-trial, that would mean a second time he'd have to come to court. And then a third time for the trial. Why would he want to keep coming back to court? If he didn't show, there'd be an arrest warrant, and probably he'd get arrested at some point when he was busy doing something important. I gave him my best, rational pitch.

"No deal, junior," he said, shaking his shaggy head of greying hair. "I want my day in court."

"Jim," I tried to empathize. "I realize these are dinky charges and that it feels like you're being picked on for something minor, but you took something without paying for it. There really isn't a defense."

Jim just folded his arms and silently mouthed "no."

Alec, the newest attorney, cheered, "Atta boy, Jim. Exercise your right to trial and shut down the whole system!" But conscientious Camille commented that obstruction was not really in Jim's best interest. These were deep questions worthy of serious debate, but I held up the dill pickle from my lunch and asked to continue the tale.

Jim and I went back into the courtroom and entered a "not guilty" plea. The judge peered over his reading glasses with pursed lips and scheduled a pre-trial. As we left, we set a time for Jim to come by my office once I'd gotten the Walmart recordings of the alleged crime.

Jim's was just one of dozens of ticky-tack misdemeanors that I had to deal with. I dutifully filed documents for discovery, got the Walmart recordings, and watched them. As predicted, they showed Jim putting a sandwich in his coat pocket and walking briskly past the cashier. Any prosecutor would see it as an open-and-shut case.

Jim arrived for our scheduled meeting on a late August day under a blazing noontime sun. He looked only slightly less disheveled with wet hair and smelling of aftershave. Perhaps he was living in a shelter. He clearly had access to shower facilities, which could only help his appearance.

I showed him the film. It was grainy, and he thought it didn't look that much like him. I explained that the security officer who was monitoring the camera would come to testify that he saw the incident and immediately alerted the guard stationed at the door who then stopped Jim. Their case wasn't just the recording.

Jim changed the subject. "I stopped drinking. I'm staying at the Lighthouse Mission. They're going to help me get a job."

I smiled. "That sounds good. You won't want to have to miss work to come to court, though." I began to discuss a plea agreement with him one more time.

"No, I want my day in court," said Jim. "I want to represent myself."

That was a new twist. I told my charges how rare this was—something only mentally imbalanced defendants seemed to want to do, and Jim was not that.

I told Jim that I didn't think it was a good idea for him to self-represent when he had a right to appointed counsel. I was not insulted by Jim's desire but confused as to why he thought he could do better than we could do as a team. Despite my best efforts to dissuade him, Jim stood firm, softly pounding my desk with his hand to emphasize the strength of his feelings.

In the end, I felt somewhat relieved, as I didn't see any defense that I could put on. "You can ask the judge about representing yourself at the pre-trial," I promised. "The judge will just have to find you competent to self-represent."

"How hard is that?" asked Jim, looking a little taken aback.

"Not really that hard, Jim. Just don't show up talking to yourself or announcing prophesies or anything." I looked him straight in the eye, and he stared back with intensity. "I think you'll do fine."

The pre-trial date rolled around on a crisp fall day. Jim's desire to represent himself was the major topic at the pre-trial conference. The judge, looking sternly down from the bench, quizzed Jim on his willingness to follow the law and the court's instructions. Jim, who had arrived wearing a long-sleeved white shirt, khakis, and a tie holding up his pants, spoke respectfully to the judge. The prosecutor rolled his eyes but did not object to Jim's request. His honor ultimately agreed that Jim was competent and had a constitutional right to represent himself. He appointed me to continue as consulting counsel, which is not something I had previously seen. I was happy to be of use and eager to see how Jim's experiment would turn out.

At this point, the prosecutor himself was calling this a "chicken-shit case" in private and regretted that it was ongoing. But Jim was still not interested in a guilty plea, and having taken the position he had, the prosecutor wouldn't budge and lose face. Neither further negotiation nor dismissal was in the cards.

Between the pre-trial and the date for the trial, Jim didn't use my consultative services. When the day for trial arrived in late December, I was in the dark about what Jim had planned for his defense. Jim surprised me by showing up to court early, carrying a tattered backpack and wearing a black overcoat and a knit scarf decorated with red reindeer. He folded the coat over the chair at counsel table, revealing a crisp white shirt, navy blue pants with a belt, and a red tie worn in the traditional manner. His beard and hair, though clean, were still long and untrimmed. He looked like a prophet who had been clothed at Mr. Mac's. We greeted each other, I asked if he needed anything from me, which he declined, and I wished him luck.

The clerk did his "oye, oye" thing and called the court to order. Jim had requested a jury trial, and the first task was to select a five-person jury. No jurors were struck for cause, and the prosecutor used his preemptory strikes to eliminate a couple of young, single people. Jim didn't ask for any help in striking jurors who seemed unlikely to be fair to him, so the jury was composed of mostly retired men and housewives. This was not what I would have ordained but so be it.

The prosecutor, appearing slightly bored but dutiful, put on his case in chief. The security officer testified to observing Jim on camera, seeing him secret the sandwich in his pocket, and alerting the floor security to stop him. The floor security officer testified to stopping Jim after he had passed the cashier and to finding the sandwich in his pocket. They played the recording so the jury could see this as well. The police officer also testified, but since Jim had not admitted anything to him, and he hadn't seen anything relevant, his testimony didn't add much.

During all this testimony Jim sat quietly beside me at counsel table with his hands folded in front of him. He did not make any objections. He didn't take any notes on the legal pad I had offered him. When the judge offered him the chance to cross-examine the witnesses, he declined. I began to wonder what his plan—if any—was.

When it was Jim's turn to take the stand, he did so. However, he did not testify about the incident at Walmart's or accuse the store guard of wrenching his arm. Instead, he talked about himself. He said he had been homeless for the past ten years, having been a vet who had served in Afghanistan and who suffered from PTSD. (The prosecutor objected on the basis of relevance and—regarding the PTSD—that Jim wasn't an expert. The judge overruled the objections.) Jim said that he was now living at the Lighthouse Mission and, due to the grace of God, was sober and getting help.

Jim went on to describe the day of the incident in early June. He had been camping under the viaduct that week, but the night before, his belongings had been stolen. This included not only his sleeping bag but a jar of Skippy peanut butter and a box of saltines he had gotten from the pantry at the Cathedral of the Madeline. In short, he hadn't eaten and hadn't had anywhere to sleep that night. He was hungry. Then Jim sat silent. The judge asked Jim if he rested, and Jim said he did.

"Interesting," said Camille. "You didn't know any of that stuff about Jim, did you?" No, I admitted, I had just talked to Jim about the incident and not about himself, really.

The judge indicated it was the prosecutor's turn to cross examine. The prosecutor paused, apparently contemplating whether he should cross. But the temptation was too great, so he began. Now he became animated, perhaps excited about a verbal jousting match. He asked Jim if he "intended" to take the sandwich without paying for it. Jim said that he was very hungry, and he just intended to eat. The prosecutor asked the judge to direct the witness to simply answer the question posed, which the judge did, and then the prosecutor proceeded with a series of yes / no questions.

"You were at Walmart, correct?"

"Yes."

"And Walmart is a store that sells things, correct?"

"Correct—the wealthiest store in the country."

"And you didn't pay for the item you had in your pocket, did you?"

"No, putting a small dent in Walmart's excessive profits."

One of the jurors smirked, but the prosecutor again asked the judge to direct the witness to simply answer the questions without commentary, and the judge again told Jim to do so. The prosecutor forged forward.

"You heard the two store guards testify that it was you, did you not?"

"Yes, I heard the two store guards."

"You saw the recording today, did you not?"

"Yes."

"And that was you taking the sandwich and walking past the cashier, was it not?"

"I don't know. It didn't look much like me. And I've known many others who've done likewise."

At that point the prosecutor evidently decided the cross examination was not going anywhere and abruptly told the judge that he rested. The judge called a short recess and explained that closing arguments would follow—the prosecutor first and last, and the defense in between.

Jim stepped down from the witness stand and came over to me. I asked if he had any questions about his closing. Was there anything he would like me to do to help? He thanked me for all the support I'd given him thus far and said he didn't think he needed anything more. I couldn't think what support I'd offered and began to wonder if this had all been a hopeless exercise in self-expression.

Jim sat down beside me at counsel table. He fumbled under the table and extracted a worn Bible from his backpack. He turned to a page marked with a purple ribbon.

The prosecutor's closing was direct and to the point. He went over the elements of "retail theft" and pointed out all the evidence that showed Jim was guilty of that crime, referencing the recording and the testimony of the two Walmart guards. He asked for a verdict of guilty.

The judge indicated that Jim could give his closing from the podium, as the prosecutor had done.

Jim walked up and put the Bible on the podium. He was silent for a moment, as if trying to collect himself or offering a prayer. Then he began to read:

"Matthew 12:1-4. At that time, Jesus went on the Sabbath day through the corn; and his disciples were hungry, and began to pluck the ears of corn, and to eat. But when the Pharisees saw it, they said unto him, 'Behold, thy disciples do that which is not lawful to do upon the Sabbath day.' But he said unto them, 'Have ye not read what David did, when he was hungry, and they that were with him; how he entered into the house of God, and did eat the shewbread, which was not lawful for him to eat, neither for them which were with him, but only for the priests?'"

I was impressed. I had not heard a defense of retail theft based on the argument that Jesus, his disciples, and David had all committed the same crime when they were hungry. The jurors were shifting in their seats looking at one another. Apparently, this was not a scenario they had seen on TV crime shows either.

Jim paused and located a red ribbon a few pages away in his Bible. He began to read again:

"Matthew 25:31. When the Son of man shall come in his glory, and all the holy angels with him, then shall he sit on the throne of his glory: And before him shall be gathered all nations: and he shall separate them one from another, as a shepherd divideth his sheep from goats: And he shall set the sheep on his right hand, but the goats on the left. Then shall the King say unto them on his right hand, 'Come, ye blessed of my Father, inherit the kingdom prepared for you from the foundation of the world: For I was hungry and ye gave me meat; I was thirsty, and ye gave me drink; I was a stranger, and ye took me in; naked and ye clothed me; I was sick, and ye visited me; I was in prison, and ye came unto me.'

Then shall the righteous answer him saying, 'Lord, when saw we thee hungry and fed thee? Or thirsty and gave thee drink? When saw we thee a stranger and took thee in? Or naked and clothed thee? Or when saw we thee sick, or in prison, and came unto thee?'

And the King shall answer and say unto them, 'Verily I say unto you, Inasmuch as ye have done it unto one of the least of these my brethren, ye have done it unto me.'"

Jim's argument that Walmart should feed him if the Waltons wanted to go to heaven was novel as well. Maybe having all these old folks on the jury was a good thing. They were looking back and forth between the judge and prosecutor, and the prosecutor was wobbling between sitting and standing, trying to decide whether he should object to some aspect of Jim's closing argument.

Jim stopped and bowed his head briefly. Then, he located a gold ribbon and turned the pages of the Bible yet again. "Jury— ladies and gentlemen of the jury. Thank you for listening to the word of God. This last verse is from Amos: 'Let justice roll down like waters and righteousness like an ever-flowing stream.'" With that Jim walked back to his seat, placed the Bible on the table in front of him, and folded his hands on top of it.

The prosecutor fumbled with the papers in front of him—then strode to the podium for his final closing words. He straightened his tie and rebuttoned his still too-tight suit jacket. I was exceedingly curious about what he would say in response to Jim's Bible lesson.

"Ladies and gentlemen of the jury," he began. "As the judge will charge you, you are to follow the law and return a verdict based on the law and the evidence. You are not to be swayed by bias or prejudice or sympathy or emotion. You are to follow the law as it is read to you. You are not to decide what you think is fair or just. Instead, it is your duty to simply follow the law." Throughout this shortest of closings, the prosecutor was not making eye contact with the jurors, and they were not making eye contact with him.

The judge then read the final instructions to the jury, and they filed out of the courtroom to deliberate.

As we waited for the jury to return, Jim walked to the back of the courtroom and began talking to an older man in a worn suit, whom I discovered was from the Lighthouse Mission. I wondered what he had thought of Jim's snippy answers on cross examination and whether the closing had been part of their missionary work. When I joined them, I heard him telling Jim that he should put his faith in the Lord and that "all things work together for good to them that love God."

I sat back, taking a bite out of my chocolate chip cookie and a slurp of coffee.

"So, what happened?" Bruce asked.

"Jim had been in and out of court for the prior ten years. After this trial, he was never charged with another crime." A couple of the defenders frowned. "Some years later I checked the records—no charges. And the births and deaths registry didn't list him as dead either."

Another one of the group guffawed. "Don't tell me this is about getting religion."

"The prosecutor became more willing to settle cases without excessive fines. So, maybe a little religion rubbed off on him," I said.

Alec crumpled up his brown paper bag, threw it across the room into the trash can, and protested. "No really. What was the outcome of the case?"

"The judge, too, started sentencing guys to time served rather than the automatic fines that homeless guys could no way pay." I smiled and took another sip of coffee.

The room turned restive. "Come on. What happened with the verdict? What did the jury do?" Bruce insisted.

"And what was the 'most important lesson of your career' you say you learned?" asked Alec.

"You'll remember, that despite Atticus Finch's excellent defense, the jury convicted Tom Robinson," I said. "And Tom was killed in prison."

They muttered to one another, checking their mutual memories about the novel and their fictional hero to confirm that I was correct.

"Jim wasn't jailed. Or fined." I concluded. "Perhaps a Christmas miracle."

Camille stood up and raised her diet Coke as if for a toast. "And you learned to honor the humanity of each client."

GHOST WRITER

OLIVE WOOLLEY BURT AWARDS, SECOND PLACE, FLASH FICTION: JUST WRITE

MAE THORN

anielle Hansen, the up-and-coming author of *Revenge*, died today at the age of twenty-seven. Some would say her methods for writing using AI were unethical, while others considered her a star. We'll keep you posted. Stay tuned tonight at ten for the full story." A reporter smiled into the camera beside Danielle.

"I'm dead?" Danielle asked the reporter but got no response. "I can't be dead. I have so much work to do." Her fingers were semi-transparent.

Reporters swarmed the entrance of the Computer Creativity building. The structure's glass walls reflected the cameras, creating a glow about her. Danielle stumbled among the cameras and newspeople, but none of them noticed. How much time had passed?

Her supervisor, Trevor, shuffled past the reporter, his shoulders heaving.

"Mr. Wilson?" The reporter shoved a microphone at him. "Care to say a few words "

He shook his head and sniffled. "No comment."

"You of all people must have something to say."

His brows drew together. "AI is no place for people like Danielle."

A gasp went up around the crowd, and more reporters circled him, speaking all at once.

"Isn't AI your bread and butter?"

"Aren't you more interested in 'computer creativity'? You coined the phrase."

He sighed and pushed past the reporters.

Danielle followed him, hoping to get his attention. "Trevor, it's me."

He made no sign he heard her but let himself into his BMW. She popped into the backseat. He slammed his hands against the steering wheel. "Damnit."

"Trevor, please hear me. You have to continue. Computer Creativity is your baby. Millions of people rely on you to make their lives better. It's AI at its finest. Without you, there is no novel."

Trevor's gaze found the rearview mirror, and she held her breath. Then, he backed his car out and headed for the freeway. They rode on in silence. It wasn't long before they parked in the garage of his multi-million-dollar home. It was all glass and marble. She shivered at the coldness of it all.

Trevor fetched a beer and headed to his study.

Danielle snickered. The man worked himself to death.

He started typing as soon as his fingers hit the keyboard.

She gazed over his shoulder. A story? Where was the AI? Where was Computer Creativity?

Trevor's fingers danced along the keys. The file name at the top of the screen read *Revenge*.

"He's writing my book, but he's not using AI."

She winced. He wrote for her. How much of her work was hers? She couldn't imagine he could write that quickly, and yet his fingers seemed to race against time as he wrote. He must be finishing off *Revenge* before her body was cold.

What about her last book? *Tears*? Had he written that too? With

AI, she wouldn't recognize her books. Hell, she had barely skimmed the new draft of *Revenge*.

What was Trevor getting at?

Trevor's cell rang, and he picked up on the third ring. His eyes were still glued to the screen.

"Hello?"

A muffled reply came from the phone.

"Yes, I'm almost done."

"That's my work," Danielle yelled.

More mumbled words.

"It's not as robotic as the last piece, but they'll never know the difference."

Mumbled words.

"Right. I'll send it to you this afternoon."

Danielle leaned over his shoulder. "You mean you've been working on this since before I died? How can you do this to me, Trevor? This is my life's work."

Trevor ended the call. "This will make us millions."

KICKAPOO RIVER DANCE

OLIVE WOOLLEY BURT AWARDS, SECOND PLACE, POETRY: NARRATIVE POEM

MARIE TOLLSTRUP

Kayaking, a ritual dance on water,
calls for smooth ballet moves.
Treading ancient Kickapoo Indian lands,
six explorers launch kayaks on the gushing

river named for its crooked current:
One who goes here, then there.
Flowing N, E, W, S, and doubling back
on itself, the Kickapoo acts as spirit balm.

Like ghosts of old, we stroke single file.
Great Nephew, Max, pumas river even if duped
and dunked by the flux early in our quest.
Like breathing, kayaking is body rhythm:

breathe in, forward stroke; breathe out,
backward stroke—a pulsing dance step.
The resolute Kickapoo heeds his own fancy,
setting up a test of wills: ageless river

versus me, novice eighty-year-old Great Aunt.
With counter-intuitive back strokes,
capricious river sweep, lurking sandbars,
the rookie-confused kayaker pirouettes

down river, sailing rapids backwards.
The Kickapoo leads as dance partner,
his whims of lazy then muscular surge.
I follow suit, paddle beaded on fall-line flow.

I glide past sculpted sandstone bluffs
draped in filigree ferns and festooned moss.
Startled by a Golden Palm Warbler's call,
lulled by serene drift, a fallen tree ensnares me.

Panic pinned, I wrangle tree limbs
and pummeling rapids, but follow orders:
Duck under the tree and leap-whirl free.
Liberated, I drift in tranquil dance.

TAKING THE LONG ROAD BACK

TYPEWRITER AWARDS, SILVER
TYPEWRITER, POETRY

MICHAEL SHOEMAKER

I trekked out
in a flurry beating
hot thin dust
on the trail
burdened with the swiftness
of worry and pretense.
On the way back
there will be
no such error.

I will take time
to lean on
the old picket fence
and stare at the
far distance, at
the mist rising
above the hills
counting my brothers
the quail
bolting from the trees
to lie on

the cool damp ground
in the meadow,
tasting the tang
of wild raspberries
looking up saluting
the bottoms of daisies
listening to
the musical consonance of bees
that must also breathe
in the sweet smell
of the graciousness of grasses
to sit in playing light and shadow
almost like a laugh by the brook
with feet immersed
in cold brisk liquid-
self-transcendence.

You ask me
how to live,
this is how.

THE NEW DRESS

TYPEWRITER AWARDS, EMERALD TYPEWRITER

PAT PARTRIDGE

An intimate documentary in three voices

MADELINE

'm no fool. I knew the graying years wouldn't be some blissful drive in the autumn sunshine, the leaves golden and the road ahead wide open. I'd been through life's sharp turns, potholes, blizzards, and dead ends. And long, dark tunnels sometimes.

But I wasn't ready when Frank died.

Ready? Not even remotely.

It was cancer. So ordinary. Yet not. At least, not to me. He went fast. Pancreatic cancer. A quick killer.

It's been two years.

Yes, I still grieve, but I no longer cry. At first, I grieved about him and about us, but then it became about me. The selfishness of grief is inevitable, I think.

As soon as the first anniversary of his death passed, my friends—bridge friends, tennis friends, lunch friends—nudged me to start dating. Said I was still young. Still vibrant. Still a beauty. Still quite a catch.

I said I didn't feel like a trout. Besides, most men prefer catch and release.

Eventually they prevailed. At least Rebecca did.

REBECCA

Madeline and I go way back. We'd worked together after college at a local bank. I switched to real estate when I got my license, but I still worked at the bank when she landed Frank. She was just a teller then but smart, with beautiful green eyes and a smile customers noticed. Customers like Frank. When he brought in the deposits from his dry-cleaning business, he always got in her line. When he asked her out, of course she said yes. She'd been expecting it. They were married within a year, bought a house, and started a family. The whole enchilada of normalcy. Frank's business took off too. Eventually, he had a chain of dry cleaners.

Madeline nailed the wife role with ease. Her almost effortless touch showed in her homemaking skills, how she raised her three kids, her sharply decorated home, her beautiful clothes. She and Frank were invited to parties and threw parties too. And they sure had a good time on the dance floor.

But there were cracks. She talked about them—to me—when she'd had a few extra glasses of whatever she was drinking at the time. She said she'd composed her story and written her fate too soon. She said she could only be half herself. Said she was reconciled to it. But she wasn't really. I consoled her. And more.

MADELINE

It would be a lie to call Rebecca my best friend, although at one time we were close, intimate friends. But we've seen a lot of each other over three decades. She was a natural at real estate and was married to another realtor, Bob, for a long time. She became the one who landed the clients and made the big bucks. Some marriages can handle that competitive difference. Theirs didn't.

Back when they were still married, our families did things together, like family weekends at the lake. Couples' things too, like bridge, dinners out, occasionally dancing.

REBECCA

Madeline's husband, Frank, was ridiculously handsome until the end. He oozed charm and charisma. Tall but not too tall, with broad shoulders, dark hair that turned peppery gray, a dimpled chin, and a smile that invited a rebound smile. He flirted effortlessly with women, even in Madeline's presence, and women flirted back. Madeline wasn't stupid or naïve, but she trusted him. At least, I think she did.

MADELINE

A few weeks ago, Rebecca invited me to a social function at Saint Paul's, her church. It's Anglican. She likes the Britishness of it, she said. I hadn't been to church for a while—not since hats and high heels were the norm—but I put on a nice dress for the occasion. Nothing new, but a dress that conveyed a certain *je ne sais quoi*.

That's where she introduced me to Phillip.

PHILLIP

Rebecca had told me about Madeline. Said I would like her right away. That proved true.

I was sipping a glass of chardonnay at this charity event at Saint Paul's when Madeline walked in. She was poised, had perfect posture. But she looked a smidgen nervous. Then she smiled when she saw someone she knew, and her face lit up. She wore a light blue dress that fit her pleasant shape perfectly.

When Rebecca introduced us, I told Madeline how much I liked her dress. I said it looked like it was made for her. She smiled, said, yes, it was.

MADELINE

Phillip and I made small talk. The usual get-to-know-you pleasantries. Careers. Kids. Grandkids. He showed pictures of his grandkids. They made him laugh, he said. A good sign.

I liked his warm smile, his unpretentiousness. But what stood out were his eyes. They were Frank's eyes. They were brown, with soft eyelids and gentle wrinkles at the corners. Eyes that laughed, I thought. Eyes I liked looking into.

He was older than Frank would have been, maybe five years older. He'd been a widower for three years or so. He wasn't going to turn the heads of young women, but I could still see the outlines and shadows of his fading handsomeness.

I don't remember much else of what we talked about. But he flirted, and I flirted back. My flirting skills were rusty but, fortunately, not rusted shut. A pleasant surprise.

When he asked me out to dinner, I hesitated.

He said, *yes* is the most powerful word in the English language.

I smiled, said yes, though I knew *no* was equally powerful.

PHILLIP

I was nervous but phoned Madeline the next day to arrange our date. I suggested a very nice restaurant, one quiet enough to talk.

It has a small dance floor, I said. Maybe we can dance.

She said, oh, I love to dance.

I hung up in a cold sweat. What was I thinking?

Dancing! I'm not much of a dancer. Yeah, I grew up in the rock-and-roll era, but I was never a fan of the dance floor. Dancing felt like torture, like self-inflicted embarrassment. Maybe I could claim I had a bad leg or plantar fasciitis in my feet. Or at least hold her off until there was a slow dance.

MADELINE

I hadn't worn a new dress to the church event where I met Phillip. Why bother? But a date was different.

I can afford a new dress, any one I want, but when I was a young woman, if I wanted a new dress, I had to sew it myself. My mother taught me to sew, and by the time I was eighteen, I sewed better than she did. Beautiful clothes were still treasured back then. I saved my meager dollars from a part-time job at Penney's to buy fabric and spent uncountable hours at my Singer. I sewed slacks, blouses, skirts. But especially dresses—summer dresses, long dresses, silk dresses.

During my twenty-eight years with Frank, I kept sewing. Sometimes I sewed clothes for the kids, but it made more sense to buy them store-bought clothes they outgrew things so fast. But I sewed nice clothes for myself. Over time, I had a fabric stash from the best fabric stores in San Francisco, Chicago, New York. Even fabric from London and Paris.

I still have a closet full of stunning fabrics ready for special occasions; some days it seems like a textile museum or a mausoleum. I suspect I'll donate most of it to a charity's second-hand store, and some young woman with little money and her mom's hand-me-down Singer will think Santa has come.

Frank never complained about my hoard of fabric. He was proud of my sewing talent. My artistic eye. My attention to detail. And my body I kept in good shape to show off my couture creations. He especially liked taking the dresses off me, his wicked smile one of my rewards.

I hadn't sewed a new dress in over three years, not since before Frank started chemo. The last one was made with pale blue silk brocade, with a scooped neck to show off a pearl necklace he'd given me for our twenty-fifth. Its hem came down to just above my knees. I had nice legs then. *Do I still?*

The date with Phillip was two weeks out, and I spent the first two days studying my fabric collection. *Silly, right?* But that's what I'd done dozens of times before. Exploring, dreaming, holding the fabrics across my unclothed body, imagining me wrapped in each one. Wanting my creation to be perfect. To show off me.

I passed on anything frilly and the showier silks—the tie-dyes, paisleys, and exotic Japanese silks. In the end, I settled on a lovely teal blue silk knit that would work well with a V-neck wrap pattern that crisscrossed my breasts. Simple, elegant, appealing.

Two days later, I'd finished carefully cutting out the pieces. Measure twice, cut once, the saying goes. For both carpenters and dressmakers. Maybe for people too.

I smiled the moment I removed the cover off my Bernina—an expensive upgrade over my Singer but worth every nickel. I was nervous. Fabric can be unforgiving. Take your eyes off the needle for a second, and you can lose control. Then, you'll be ripping out errant stitches and starting over, hoping you haven't destroyed your precious fabric.

The Bernina responded to my touch with ease. Some skills you never lose.

PHILLIP

Dinner with Madeline went well. We ate at Rudolph's Steak House. White tablecloths, good service, soft lighting, the works. There was a small dance floor, but it wasn't until a jazz combo started playing that I started to worry.

Madeline looked beautiful. Simply beautiful. Everything about her was just right. Her hair. Her makeup. And a stunning teal blue dress—silk, she said—that fit her exquisitely. I'd been out with a few women over the past year, but Madeline tripped some wires inside me in unexpected ways.

We hit it off, I know she would agree. We told stories, smiled, laughed a lot. We talked while the combo played, but when they started a slow tune—a sultry version of Cole Porter's "Night and Day"—Madeline's smile brightened. That was my cue.

Would you like to dance, I asked. She, of course, said yes.

MADELINE

Sometimes small surprises can lead to bigger surprises. When Phillip and I started to dance, I knew quickly he wasn't in his element. He held me cautiously, politely, his body inches from mine. But I could still feel the heat coming off him, and he smelled good. A smell I'd missed. After a while, I looked up at him and asked, would you like me to lead? He grinned, said sure.

I pulled him closer, his chest against my breasts. I put my head on his shoulder, but I took control of our hands and guided him as we danced. He caught on quickly, seemed to relax, to enjoy himself. More than he or I expected, as it turned out.

PHILLIP

Dancing with Madeline took me to another place in my head. A much younger place. I let her lead, her chest against mine, her light perfume filling my nostrils, scrambling my brain in a most unexpected way. When the song ended, we stayed on the dance floor for the next song and then the next one, but I couldn't name the songs if my life depended on it. Her body, her movement intoxicated me. That's when I started to get an erection, the kind of good old hard-on of a much rawer me. Oh crap! I knew she'd notice. I tried to ease my body away a little, but she pulled me closer, looked at me, and winked.

MADELINE

Life is made for firsts, right? Even though it was a first date, we ended up in bed at my place. It was out of character for both of us, I'm sure, but Phillip quickly said yes when I invited him for a nightcap. I wanted him and didn't see any reason to deny myself. Why should I? It sounds promiscuous when I tell it, but *promiscuous* is just a word. Desire doesn't need words. When we'd danced and he got aroused, I felt something inside me switch on. Something primitive but wonderful. Even now, words slide by without capturing the urge I felt.

It was the first time after Frank I'd had another man in my bed, and things went well. He pulled my dress over my head, admired my body with hungry eyes. *Hungry for me.* We quickly ripped off and tossed aside the rest of our clothes like used-up gift wrapping. And when our unclothed bodies connected, he let me take the lead again, which I liked.

When the action subsided, and we lay side by side in repose, I turned to him and smiled, said it's time for you to go home.

REBECCA

Madeline is the epitome of poise, but she likes being in charge. That includes in bed. I know.

PHILLIP

I went home distracted and more than a little dazed. Madeline had been amazing in bed, her lips inviting, her breathing hard, her touch confident, her legs swirling around me.

Before I left her house, we set a date for lunch two days later. She picked a small Italian restaurant that was rather romantic for a Monday lunch. She entered wearing blue jeans and a forest-green blouse that complemented her eyes. Silk again? I asked. She smiled. Yes, she said.

I'd lost sleep trying to imagine what I was going to say to this extraordinary woman who had so boldly shared her body with me. Yet there she sat, smiling calmly, the embodiment of composure. I only knew I wanted more.

We ordered. But before our meals had even arrived, she floored me with a direct question.

Did you ever cheat on your wife? she asked.

I'm sure I blushed. But somehow lying to this woman seemed wrong. Impossible.

Yes, I said. I started to say it was a long time ago, but before I could, she said, my husband Frank did too.

Our food arrived, and when the waiter left the table, she asked if my wife knew.

I don't think so, I said.

I knew, she said. Her eyes softened, and she took a bite of her roll.

What was I going to say? Saying nothing didn't seem like an option. She seemed to invite intimacy. Confessional intimacy.

Did you know her? I asked.

Yes, she said. Oh, yes.

Then she went back to her meal. As did I. She changed the topic, and we had a delightful lunch.

I decided not to ask her if she'd ever cheated.

MADELINE

By the time you're my age, you will have abandoned many of your delusions. That's not necessarily a bad thing. But it's not without pain. Some delusions become good friends, buffering reality's harsher edges. Losing a delusion is a different kind of *petit mort,* a little death that lessens you, at least for a while.

I'd grown into my delusions. As life progressed and became easier, I'd wrapped my happiness in simple beliefs: That I'd earned my ease. Raised healthy and competent children, who now had their own broods. Turned into a fun grandma. Remained a friend to many. And loved an imperfect but loving husband.

Only weeks before Frank's diagnosis, he and I were planning all the ways we'd enjoy our later years doing things we'd enjoyed for decades. Travel, hold family reunions, play bridge, watch the Broncos, go dancing.

Definitely, we'd go dancing. We made a sharp couple on the dance floor, everyone said. Whoever wrote that dancing is a vertical expression of a horizontal desire—they got it right. Frank and I loved sex after a night dancing. One seemed to flow into the next.

Desire, passion, intimacy—they're not easy to corral. One day you believe your sex life is all about love and companionship and commitment. And then you discover secrets. Sometimes the secrets are yours to keep. But sometimes, like an old dress, no longer worth holding onto.

When Phillip rose from the bed after our first night together, I studied his aging body. Could be worse, could be better, I calculated. As he dressed, I pulled on a robe and escorted him to the door. We kissed good night, of course.

After he left, I poured myself a glass of ice-cold Coke—my longstanding treat after sex. It tasted wonderful. Then, I headed back to bed.

My beautiful new teal blue dress that had wrapped my body so perfectly lay in a crumpled pile on the floor. I picked it up and examined it. There was a stain on it, still moist.

Ruined? Hardly.

THE BARK PARK

OLIVE WOOLLEY BURT AWARDS, FIRST
PLACE, NEW VOICES: GENERAL & LITERARY
FICTION

SHEENA BLANKENAGEL

The coppery red cliffs of Sedona are looming over me, accusatory glares etched along their russet faces. The shadowed crags and jutted outcroppings shoot a lance of yearning through my chest, and I look away, shoving the pain down where it belongs. No time to indulge in the bittersweet pangs of longing right now.

Buddy's eyes are sparkling with excitement, shoulders rolling beneath tawny fur as we approach the gate to The Bark Park. As the latch opens, a roiling tussle of happy dogs greets us, clobbering my pup with excited pounces and wet noses. Letting out a happy woof, he tumbles away with the turbulent mass of fur.

The dog is getting exercise—check. One more task I can scrape off my list. Inside the enclosed field, benches are littered with dog park people. Some throw an occasional ball while the rest stare vacantly at their phones. At least one of the picnic tables is free, and I plow toward it, eyes on my sneakers.

"Hey, Jean." A bespectacled woman is waving at me, bohemian skirts drifting in the autumn breeze.

Crap. The small talk we've traded hasn't exactly seared her name in my memory.

"Hey there." I throw her a smile without lingering eye contact.

My laptop is heavy on my shoulder, tugging me to the table like a needle pointed north. Anchoring in, I spread my notes and bags across the space, limiting the available real estate to send a clear message: *I'm not available to chat.* Deadlines are imprinted on the backs of my eyelids as I insert my ear buds and stare drearily at the screen that rules my life.

Vaguely, I'm aware of dog owners coming and going, new pups careening into the field. On the other side of the park is the small dog area, serving an albeit overgeneralized demographic of seniors. My nose crinkles at them, leaning into each other with engrossed conversation. They must not have a giant to-do list, retired from the interminable wheel of society that circulates with the sweat, tears, and sleepless nights of those of us still trapped within. Must be *nice.*

Before succumbing to my keyboard, I snatch a glance at others. The ball throwers are gone, and the rest appear just as detached from the present as I am. They too drown in their screens, not surfacing for breath. A begrudging realization rides up my spine.

I am just as jacked in as they are. Just as entangled as those other automatons in the day-to-day grind, plugging through each task only to make it to the next. Frustration swells into a malignant shadow, engulfing my focus.

When did I get this way? When did life become a monotony of redundant obligations? Make breakfast, shuffle kids to the bus, tap tap tap in the emails, buy the groceries, make dinner, bath time. Rinse, lather, repeat.

I let out a disgruntled sigh. Too big of an existential question to contemplate right now. I'll do some soul searching on that one later, after I get some of these files off my desk.

Soon, I'm checked out of the real world, lost in my tangle of messy inboxes and files, when the sound of gravel crunching beneath wheels snaps me out of the laser beam I'm staring into my computer. Seated atop a motorized wheelchair, a middle-aged woman approaches the gate with her dog.

The cacophony of barking and claws on concrete accosts every newcomer as the rowdy pack swarms the gate, tails whipping with glee. It's the same gymnastics challenge for all of us, trying to usher our dog in without letting the others out, all while being mauled by happy balls of fur.

Watching the woman, I unfold myself from the picnic table. Does she need help getting in? None of the other dog park people give her a second glance, and I hesitate. She exhibits no sign of needing assistance.

The least I can do is herd the dogs away from the gate. Letting out a whistle and waving a ball, I lure the horde so she can roll in. Her dog soon joins the pack, bouncing on overlong juvenile legs. I stand close enough to help if needed but far enough away to not hover. Why didn't anyone else come to see if she needs help?

"That's Rowdy." She looks at me, pride gleaming from her eyes as she points a bony finger at her dog. "Labradoodle."

As we engage in the obligatory dog park introduction of discussing breeds and temperament, my eyes are shifting back to my camp. I've got to finish that email. How do I make a graceful exit?

"I'm Amanda," she says. With the press of a finger, she propels forward, chair whirring like a bumblebee trapped in a jar.

November is still shorts weather, and I take in her skeletal legs, patellas protruding from atrophied muscle like overgrown burls on an oak tree.

"I'm Jean."

Her wheels are spitting gravel as she tries to climb the lip of the sidewalk.

"Can I help?" I ask hesitantly.

"Nope. Just need to get a run at it." She's reversing at an alarming rate, hits the throttle, and pops up onto the concrete.

"I see why they call this red rock country," Amanda says. "Can you believe the way the Aztec sandstone flames against the blue sky?" She rolls to a stop at my table then pushes a button to recline in her chair. "I used to love rock climbing. Looks like there's some good anchors on that chimney."

I can't help the grimace that pinches my face. I moved to Sedona for its glut of mountain biking trails that beckon riders from all over the country. There's no better feeling than tires gripping sandstone, the full body heat wave from shredding the downslope. Now though, I go out of my way to avoid studying the rusty cliffs surrounding my home. It hurts too damn much that my bike is collecting dust in a storage unit while I'm stuck on my laptop all day. The only thing that takes the sting out is reminding myself that someday—*someday*—I'll have the time to go out and bomb the trails. Later.

"Rock climbing, huh?" I need to get back to work but can't resist the pull of her smile. It's huge and genuine, set against hollow cheeks below her sunglasses.

"Oh, yeah. I used to love all that crazy stuff. Whitewater kayaking, longboarding competitions, you name it."

"Wow," I mutter, torn between jealousy and fascination.

"Hard to believe a mosquito did this to me."

My eyes snap down to her emaciated arms and crooked fingers. An instant reel of news stories plays like a patchy documentary in my head. What was that virus called again? I open my mouth to respond, but she beats me to it.

"West Nile." Amanda shrugs. "Four years ago, at Willow Lake."

Blown away by her nonchalant grin, I shove my hands in my pockets. "Jeez."

"Yeah, my climbing buddies couldn't believe it. Said, 'after all the crazy shit you've done Amanda, how could it be a *mosquito* that finally took you out?'"

The illusory pull of my computer evaporates, deadlines forgotten. She's chuckling, and I crack an incredulous smile. How can she be so lighthearted?

"I was in a coma for four months. I always tell people the worst words you could ever hear are 'blink once for yes, twice for no.'"

An ache of sympathy rolls over me, tightening my gut. "Four months? That's insane."

Why can't I think of anything appropriate to say? Should I go for something positive? Motivational? I breathe a silent sigh of relief when she continues, my mouth quirking into an affectionate smile. She is enchantingly chatty.

"Had a fever of 107 for over a week," she chuckles. "The brain dies at 107.6. They kept trying to get my husband to pull the plug. Said if I ever woke up, I'd be brain dead."

"Wow, that must have been so hard." Validation is what I settle for. "I'm sorry you had to go through that."

"Spent a year in the hospital before I could finally walk again." Amanda shifts her shoes against the footpad and nods at our dogs tumbling in the grass. "I've got it pretty good though. I can still drive Rowdy to the park and get myself in and out of this chair."

I tend to not be an overly emotional person, but now my throat is tightening, and I have to blink a couple times. Her entire life was turned upside down by a freaking bug and she says she's got it good?

"Do you think you'll continue to improve or…?" I let the question fizzle. Crap, was that insensitive to ask?

In the space of a heartbeat, before she answers, hope rakes against discomfort in my chest. I'm imagining Amanda webbed in climbing gear against the face of a cliff, defined muscles cut sharp beneath a sheen of sweat. If she went from a coma to walking, maybe someday she can get back to climbing?

"Nah," she says. The softness of her smile cuts me to the quick. "I see a small development every once in a while, but I think this is pretty much it."

"Oh." Disappointment flushes through me.

"I'd like to train Rowdy as a service dog. They have those handles dogs wear. He could help me balance when I walk."

We both laugh aloud when Rowdy leaps like a goofy gazelle and then rolls into a wrestling match with Buddy. Amanda looks at me then, probably noticing my failed attempt not to appear dispirited.

"I could have been much worse off." Amanda closes her eyes, soft creases of her face gilded in sunlight. "I sure miss climbing though."

"Well, it's truly incredible you have such a beautiful outlook on life," I say.

It's been a long time since I met anyone as impressive as Amanda, and my mind is spinning with comparisons. If I wound up in a wheelchair, would I be so positive? Or would I cycle into a depressed whirlpool of self-pity? I resist the superstitious urge to knock on something made of wood as my fearful imaginings run rampant.

"My life is good, and I've done some really awesome things. You know, a lot of people wait until they retire to start enjoying their lives. I sure am glad I didn't. I would've missed everything."

I'm reeling, both from amazement and panic. How many more ledges had Amanda wanted to conquer, only to have her plans of adventure pitched into the tumble cycle to come out wrinkled and shrunken? It's terrifying how quickly everything can change.

The reminder of life's fragility is a surreal slap to the face, flushing my cheeks. I glance at my dog, his pink tongue lolling. Do I ever even appreciate his unconditional love? Do I ever take time to truly appreciate all the amazing things in my life?

As the sun settles lazily against the horizon, it armors the red rock with the glow of freshly forged bronze. Rather than appreciating the beauty and opportunity all around me, I've been dozing through each day in a trance of monotony.

A rush of gratitude burns low in my chest. I have a beautiful, loving family at home. A body that does everything I ask it to. Enough money to make ends meet. And I have time. Time to spend however I choose. I can shuffle things around and do them later. Or… I can do them now.

Amanda snaps me out of my reverie. "I figured it out, you know."

"Oh yeah?" My curiosity piques at her playful smile.

"Yep. Right before I was hospitalized, I started a pest control company." She's appraising me, but I'm not sure what response she's waiting for. I simply arch an eyebrow and wait.

"I'll tell ya, those mosquitos knew what I was up to. They banded together and came after me." Her hoot of laughter echoes across The Bark Park. My stunned chuckle joins hers, and a few dogs perk an ear, cocking their heads.

An hour speeds by. Our chatter is infused with Amanda's wry sense of humor, and I can't stop laughing. As sunset begins to rob the sky of color, I check my watch. Time to get the kids from soccer.

"It was awesome to meet you," I tell Amanda. My heart is so warm, I don't want to leave. We could probably yammer for days without running out of things to say.

"You too. See ya tomorrow." She waves and smiles then rolls over to a nearby dog owner to compliment them on their poodle's fancy haircut.

Later, my daughters are chattering songbirds in the backseat as I ponder on the way I spend my time. These thoughts have crowded all else from my head since I left the dog park. If everything got stripped away tomorrow, would I be pleased with the way I'd lived my life?

In my mind's eye, I see the framed quote hanging above my coffee machine. *"I'd rather live with regret than wonder."*

I'd bought it a hundred years ago at some gas station in the Midwest because it seemed like the perfect mantra for my life. In younger years, I'd always been the type to take risks, rail the biggest berms, and clean the gnarliest trails. In so few words, that quote perfectly condensed the way I'd rather shralp the trail, and perhaps regret it, than be left with the terrifying alternative. A life spent wondering what heights I could have reached if I hadn't chickened out.

Sheesh. What happened to that younger me?

With a glance in the rearview, I see the beautiful, bright-eyed faces of my girls. The hair on my arms prickles as a new thought rolls over me. What message do I want to model for my kids? That adulthood is a monotonous grind of to-dos? Or that time is precious, and in truth, can be spent any way we desire?

My youngest is giggling, pressing a round fingertip to the window.

"Uh, you missed the turn to our house," she says.

"I know, baby." I roll my shoulders, filling my lungs fully for the first time in ages. "We're heading to the storage unit. First though, I think we should stop at Red Mountain Cycle. How do you girls feel about learning to mountain bike?"

THREADING THE NEEDLE

TYPEWRITER AWARDS, GOLD TYPEWRITER,
POETRY

SUSAN J. WURTZBURG

Purple cotton-polyester, like my father,
blend of nature and artifice. Thoughtful
threads interwoven with aggressive
brightness. This dress shirt, Singapore made,
his father's city. Shipped across the ocean,
like his pater, but in hull, not cabin-class. Stiff-collared
British formal-style attire, my dad, at times.

Ancient, soft fabric,
more flexible than my father,
outlived his mind, lost at sea,
in the muddy blitzed depths.
Followed by his body, strand
by strand, unraveled in the end.

This cloth relic, worn by me,
by the ocean, sun shelter.
Faded colors, like my memories,
much mislaid, murky mysteries.

JAKE

OLIVE WOOLLEY BURT AWARDS, FIRST
PLACE, SPIRITUAL ESSAY
THOMAS I. WAHL

ake was like a grandfather to me.

He had what he called a low German accent, although I had never heard him speak German. Jake didn't talk much about immigrating from his homeland except that he liked Kaiser Wilhelm. Jake had a full head of grey hair, always wore bib overalls, loved beer, and was a chain smoker.

Jake and I would walk through the hog barns each morning, checking the pigs, feeders, and waterers. Hog barns are dusty and have a strong odor—they stink. Once outside, Jake would cough and cough and cough, eventually spitting out some goop.

"That's from smoking," he'd say.

He never told me not to smoke, but I never did.

Jake taught me to drive a tractor on an old Farmall M. No power steering and a very stiff clutch, or at least stiff for a ten-year-old. At first, Jake sat in the seat behind me.

"Step on the clutch. Put it in first gear. Make sure the brakes are off. Let the clutch out slowly. Feel where it starts to engage Watch where you are going. Easy on the brakes."

Once I got the hang of driving around the farmyard, Jake stood on the drawbar behind me until he thought it was safe to drive by myself.

"First gear only around the farmyard."

Eventually, he let me drive the tractor in the field. Cultivating corn at two miles per hour is exciting at first, but boring after a few hours. I don't think Jake liked cultivating. Is that why he taught me to drive a tractor?

Jake let me drive the pickup out to the field and back when I was about thirteen or fourteen. As far as I know, he didn't tell my father. Jake always had my back.

One of the worst summertime jobs was baling straw. It was dirty and usually hot enough to cause sunstroke. After stacking straw bales in the barn all day, we would sit on the lawn covered in dust and sweat. Okay, maybe not Dad or Jake, but my younger brothers and I certainly were.

Dad brought out a cold six-pack of Pabst Blue Ribbon. I got to taste it. I didn't particularly like it, but it was the grown-up thing to do. Dad and Jake enjoyed it. I still don't care for PBR.

The next day, a neighbor called needing help baling straw. Rain was in the forecast. My job was to stack the heavy rectangles on the hay wagon as the baler relentlessly spit them out in the hundred-degree heat of August.

As we circled the field, the baler gobbled up the ribbon of straw and compressed it into bales. I stacked the bales inter-locking on the rocking and bouncing hay wagon. I lasted two loads. A gulp from the jug of ice water made me sick. Barf sick. I was dizzy—my first experience with heat exhaustion.

The neighbor brought me home. Jake made me hold my wrists under the cold water from the faucet in the yard to cool me off.

"Never dunk your head under the cold water right away, only your wrists so you cool off slowly."

Jake made me lie in the shade of an apple tree in the yard and gave me some whiskey. It smelled awful and tasted worse.

"Drink this. It will thin your blood and help cool you off." It burned all the way down my throat, but I guess it helped.

I was done stacking bales for the day. I never stacked bales on the hay wagon behind the baler again. And Jake never gave me whiskey again.

Jake liked his beer on the weekends, mostly light lagers like PBR. A few miles away across the border in Minnesota, bars were open on Sundays. When I got my learner's permit, I chauffeured Jake to Minnesota on Sunday afternoons for a few hours. It was a good experience for me, even though Jake wouldn't let me go over forty-five miles per hour in his pride and joy, a 1959 blue, six-cylinder, three-speed, four-door Chevy. Maybe his only possession of value.

I heard many stories as a sixteen-year-old sitting in a bar drinking pop for a few hours. Yes, it's pop, not soda, in the upper Midwest. Jake would drink a few PBRs or whatever was cheap. He didn't talk much. I think he was an introvert at heart.

"You learn more by listening," he said on the way home. He explained some of the stories, what was BS, and who was full of it. Sorting the wheat from the chaff is a life skill.

By the time I started farming on my own, Jake was retired. He would stop by occasionally to chat, help out, and maybe give advice, but only if asked. More life lessons.

When my first child, Michelle, was born, Jake had to hold her when we brought her home. For Michelle's second birthday, he bought her a tiny set of bib overalls with a railroad engineer cap. There are pictures somewhere. Jake was family.

Jake moved to a small town about an hour away, and I didn't see him often. A few years later, he quit driving and gave me his Chevy. As a Ford fan, I didn't appreciate the Chevy as much as I should have. It became a demolition derby car after sitting around for a few years.

When I quit farming, we moved to Ames, and I went back to school. Jake moved into a nursing home. The nursing home didn't have my new contact information. I didn't find out until months later that Jake had passed on to that great beer hall in the sky.

When I finally visited his grave, the groundskeeper said not many folks came by looking for Jake's resting place.

I sobbed quietly as I thought about everything Jake had done for me.

Jake was a grandfather to me, and I still miss him.

I think that he would have liked my homebrew and stories.

MYSTERIOUS UNIVERSE

OLIVE WOOLLEY BURT AWARDS, FIRST
PLACE, NEW VOICES: POETRY

TIMOTHY DOYLE

We are infatuated
with the big and inconceivably far,
the deep, cool wells of telescopes,
insect-like, gold-foiled spaceships,
necklaces of galaxies, planets, and stars.

Yet, a few miles from our front door
lies that most mysterious,
most improbable universe
that we unmindfully ignore,
poison, annihilate, and pave.

A glistening garnet wasp
orbits a wild rose
with diaphanous, auroral wings.
A praying mantis stalks prey,
mechanical yet greenly alive.

Blackberries, like globular clusters—
salmon pink, goldfish orange,
ruby and amethyst—
cook sweet, complex molecules
in bright August heat.

Embedded within
leafy, dark-green nebulae
of Oregon grape
lay scattered yellow suns
the size of ladybugs.

Orb weavers cast
spiraling magnetic lines.
Monarch butterflies
crowd the edge of a drying puddle,
wings pulsing like stellar atmospheres.

The murmuring canyon brook
and crystalline birdsong
from humid canopy shadows
sing a melody more indecipherable
than any pulsar's voice.

FROM RUSSIA, WITH BORSCHT

TYPEWRITER AWARDS, GOLD TYPEWRITER, NONFICTION

INNA V. LYON

MARCH 2003

check my watch for the 10th time—three hours and fifteen minutes before boarding. The merciless departure time is approaching fast. The moment Seryozha and I step over that line at the security checkpoint of the Sheremetyevo International Airport, our lives will change forever. Shudders run through my body, and I clench-unclench my fists a few times. Spending a month in a hospital—where they patched my stomach after a case of internal bleeding—hadn't helped my nerves to settle down.

"Inna, are you listening?" my mother asks me.

"What? What did you ask?" I reply with a question.

"Will you give me a call when you guys arrive in Salt Lake City?"

"Yes, of course I will. As soon as I find out if they have a landline or cell phone, figure out the time difference with Russia, the long-distance call rates, and how long I can be on the phone."

Mom tries to smile but wipes her eyes instead.

Russian superstitions say that on the first part of a trip, you think about what you left behind, and during the second part, what lies ahead. March 26th, 2003, proves them wrong. All I can think about is how to get us—my eleven-year-old son Seryozha and I—to our new home in Salt Lake City, Utah, USA. Later, I would worry about what I left behind.

I have never been anywhere outside of Russia, and I have no idea how to get around Sheremetyevo, the biggest airport I've ever seen—to say nothing of the looming challenge of JFK. I stutter every time I open my mouth and speak English to someone. I have no experience going through security or talking to border patrol officers. My catchphrase, "Please, speak slowly," might not get me far. All I have with me is a Russian-English pocket dictionary, a folder thick with paperwork, a few dollar bills, and US visas in our passports. Our simple belongings fit into a huge colorful suitcase that my son will be lugging around since I have weight restrictions from my doctors. And I have hope. Hope that somehow, we will find family, friends, and a home in that new faraway land.

"Inna, dear, we will see each other again." My sister squeezes my hand in hers.

I nod. Tears in my throat, I squawk "yes," not believing that it will ever happen. I don't have the luxury of crying for my mom's sake. The determination in her eyes to tear our airline tickets to pieces—canceling the whole ordeal of international marriage on the spot—is too obvious.

"Mom, it's been fifteen minutes. We need to go."

Seryozha comes back from exploring the nearby shops. He acts just like a kid who is excited to be on a plane for the first time.

Trying to hide my jitters, I get up. All goodbyes are spoken. All hugs are given multiple times. No more borrowed minutes being with my loved ones, I grab Seryozha's hand in mine, my carry-on bag in another, and take my first step into a new life.

———

The eight-hour flight from Moscow to New York feels like an eternity.

The newspapers passed around by the flight attendants are still in Russian. So are the movies in our personal consoles in front of us. But everything else is so foreign, and I don't understand half of what people around me are saying. I want to hide inside my heavy fur coat's hood and sob for a few minutes.

But Seryozha is too excited to miss even a minute of our new adventures. He turns to me. "I almost peed my pants when the plane took off. Mom, we are going to fly over the ocean. Just imagine if the plane breaks—we will be swimming in the cold water."

I'd rather not imagine that, or I, too, will pee my pants.

Seryozha presses the button to call a flight attendant.

"Can I please have tomato juice?" he asks. The flight attendant smiles and brings him two boxes of juice.

We eat something, ordering food in English. We stand in line for the airplane bathroom. Seryozha begs me for money and buys something from the catalog of useless merchandise. Spoken English is deafening to me. Mom, why didn't you tear my tickets? Will I ever again feel the warmth of your embrace and hear familiar Russian speech?

Getting through the US border is turning into humiliation. Despite our rigorous English lessons, the customs control officer doesn't understand us. He calls for an interpreter's help over the phone.

"Czy rozumiesz język polski?"

The Polish interpreter has enough vocabulary to understand that even though I'm already the wife of a US citizen, we are coming on a fiancé visa. The process takes over forty minutes before we hear the hackneyed phrase, "Welcome to America," with the desired thud of a stamp in our passports.

The JFK airport overwhelms us with its size, colors, and indifference to its two small, tired Russian passengers. Unknown smells, multinational crowds, signs, flashy billboards, and mumbled announcements—all in English, too fast to read or understand. Too big. Too noisy. Too unfamiliar.

"Mom, I want to buy something. I want to do it myself."

Seryozha makes it a goal to spend our last twenty-dollar bill on food and drinks. A bottle of Coke and a box of cookies take it all. Converted into Russian rubles, that twenty would've bought us our weekly groceries.

The five-hour layover in JFK and the following four-and-a-half-hour flight to Salt Lake City drains the last of our energy. It is nighttime in Russia, and we zone out as soon as we find our seats on the back of the airplane to Salt Lake. No drink or snack could keep us awake.

I think about how we need to go through another custom border embarrassment and look around. But, alas, no mean border watchdogs, fast English questions, or quick fingers going through our paperwork. We keep moving along with other passengers.

"Mom, how much longer?"

I have the same question. All we want is to lie down and close our eyes for a good ten hours.

My bag gets heavier with every step. Seryozha checks on me often, but day-long exhaustion takes over my son. He falls to his knees in the middle of the airport's hallway. I pick him up, thankful for the carpeted floor. Even Moscow's fanciest international airport has only tiled floors. America blows my mind with its monstrosity and weird customs.

A welcoming hug from my American husband Paul and his youngest daughter Laila relieves me of the duty of getting us overseas. We have made it. We are here. America is our new home. So why do my tears taste bitter?

———

The first couple of days upon our arrival to Utah, all we want to do is sleep.

In the morning, Seryozha and I put on brave faces, but by noon, fatigue takes over. We both crawl back to our beds.

At the end of our second day, my husband's sister, now my sister-in-law, brings us two dishes—chicken and rice casserole and apple pie. I find them plain and boring, but she lets me keep the fancy blue glass dishes as a welcoming present.

On the third day, my son and I break into hives from the change in climate and unfamiliar food and water. The cortisone cream only makes us sleepier.

"You have to stay awake," says my husband. "It is called *jet lag*, and it will go away if you try to adjust to American time."

Easy for him to say. We'd never flown that far nor experienced so many time zone changes.

Seryozha thinks that jet lag translates into "airplane feet," and so we shake our feet as often as we can the next day. It helps. Or maybe our curiosity about the new country takes over, and we brave the daylight.

On Friday, my husband takes us to our first American restaurant: Hometown Buffet. Its variety blows my mind—Chinese, Italian, Mexican, a salad bar, roast beef, all kinds of fish, breads, even beef liver with onions, desserts, and ice cream stations.

My husband is eating tacos. The Seryozha's plate has mountains of mashed potatoes. I have a bit of everything that looks exotic. To my disappointment, the food doesn't taste as good as it looks. It is missing something. It has enough seasoning, fat, and sweetness, but it lacks real taste. I don't know exactly what's wrong with it, but even after I'm full, I don't feel satisfied.

I'm a foodie. I'm a cook. I think that a country and culture are best learned through its cuisine. American food tastes like cardboard.

I see my husband's worried look, eyeing my untouched plate.

I love him for his worry, kindness, dedication, and concern.

I don't like America, and I don't like its food.

APRIL-MAY 2003

A week after our arrival, the first week of April, my husband takes me to ESL, the English as a Second Language school, to study English. I pass the placement test and join the mid-level group. We study grammar and conversation. It turns out that my English is not so bad. There are many people there from South America, Mexico, and Brazil; they keep to themselves. There is no one from Russia. I am alone. School is boring, unfamiliar, and complicated. I can't say I enjoy it.

Over the next two months, Seryozha and I get into some mischief while adjusting to our new life.

I never had a dishwasher before and failed to learn that nothing except dishwasher detergent could be used for the machine. The washing machine detergent looks the same thing to me. The kitchen floor is spotless after that experience.

Seryozha warms up a baked potato, still wrapped in aluminum foil, in the microwave, causing a small explosion that led my husband to buy a new microwave, along with the pleasure of installing it himself.

I find American desserts too sweet but fail trying to bake my signature honey cake. My time-tested recipe doesn't work. Even honey is different. I don't know whom to blame—the oven, the American ingredients, or a clumsy baker. I spend several frustrating hours, and as a result, the hard-as-a-rock cake goes into the garbage.

I bake another cake for our neighbor Elizabeth who gives Seryozha and me piano lessons once a week. Little do I know that using raw egg whites whipped with sugar is not common for cake frosting in America. My beautifully decorated cake is given to the neighbors who, rumor has it, take a bunch of pictures but don't eat it fearing Salmonella contamination.

Seryozha hates all American cheese, complaining that it tastes like sawdust.

At the family party, my husband's brother Lowell challenges me to try a bloody hamburger, and I scream after taking the first bite, seeing blood dripping onto my plate. Clueless Lowell kills my craving for classic American meals forever.

I refuse to eat hamburgers anywhere, and to my husband's dismay, I eat just hamburger buns as bread with any meal.

I start calling my son Seryozha only by his full name, Sergey. Seryozha is too tongue-twisting for the Americans. His short name is too private and dear to me. I reserve it for our rare conversations in Russian.

JUNE 2003

Now it is summer break at ESL, and I'm in a different school—A-1 driving school—with a bunch of fifteen-year-old teenagers. They already know how to drive. After walking to the post office in 104-degree heat, I know I want to learn how to drive.

My husband Paul comes back from a business trip to Washington. I'm fascinated that there are two of them—Washington State and the capital, Washington DC. I didn't know that.

On Saturday, Paul invites all three of us—Sergey, Laila, and me —to visit Larissa, his Russian tutor, who has given him a few language lessons in the past. Larissa moved to the US from Russia about ten years ago. She works as a clerk at a retail store and occasionally gives Russian lessons. Paul's vocabulary of four words— "love, husband, pillow, and blanket"—make me doubt Larissa's tutoring skills.

Larissa lives in a fancy downtown apartment with access to a gym and a swimming pool. We meet her in the lobby. Light green capris and a white T-shirt fit her petite figure like a glove. She is blonde and chatty. I feel a pang of jealousy when Larissa and my husband hug each other. I still can't understand this American greeting. In Russia, you only hug people you know well. Do they know each other well? I will find out later. Now I hang onto each word and try to convince myself that I'm not jealous.

"Inna, you came to America in March, right?" asks Larissa. "How do you like it here, and what was your first impression?" she asks in English with a heavy Russian accent. Do I speak like that, too?

"It's fine," I lie.

On our way here, my husband called Larissa's apartment "a little Russia." Now I see why. Her two-bedroom apartment looks like any Russian home: Russian books on the shelves, Russian nesting dolls lining the table, and wall posters with Alla Pugacheva, a Russian singer. Larissa turns down the blaring TV with a movie in (of course) Russian language and points to her couch.

"Sit."

Russians are very hospitable, and I expect some food to be served to us guests. Larissa offers only pistachio ice cream. Sergey and I love it. I need to find out where she buys it.

"I go buy ice cream at Albertsons. It is really good and yummy. I add more pee-sta-chios," says Larissa, answering my thoughts. "I think they—what that word—oh, greedy—when they do not put more nuts."

Larissa speaks English with a heavy accent and misses her articles. I realize that is how I speak. After three months in America, Sergey's English is much better than both of us combined. My son has a knack for languages. Oh, and he plays video games with his friends all the time. Sonic and Zelda rule.

A few minutes later, Larissa's daughter shows up. Larissa's carbon copy has the same name—Larissa. But college student Larissa has much better English than her mother and much worse manners. She greets us, gives us a lopsided smile, and slams the door to her bedroom. I get the vibe that the daughter does not approve of her mother inviting Russian friends over. I want to know their story.

———

We take turns changing into bathing suits in a tiny bathroom and go to the indoor community pool.

"Mom, Laila, watch me diving," yells Sergey before anyone can warn him of the sign on the wall: "No diving." Too late. Splash. Boom. Sergey cannonballs into the middle of the pool, sending an array of cold water onto the rest of the party. I laugh, looking at our wet company.

"Ouch, I'm wet," complains Laila.

"Well, you'll get wet eventually if you are getting in the water," reasons my husband.

The water is fresh and pleasant. Larissa and my husband chat in the lounge chairs. Sergey wants to do it all—noodle fighting, Marco Polo, and pretending he is a walrus, slipping off the pool's edge into the water, making it look like a not-too-splashy cannonball.

I like the pool, but I want to leave and take my husband away from Larissa, who pats his hand too casually.

On our way home, the car's air smells like chemicals. Larissa told us to take our showers at home. She didn't have towels for all of us. Sergey plays on his Gameboy, and Laila listens to her iPod.

"Did you like Larissa?" asks my husband.

"I like ice cream," I answer too fast.

What is going on? Am I jealous? I sigh.

"She is fine. How many times did she give you Russian lessons?" The question has been on my mind since morning when my husband announced our visit downtown.

"Only a couple of times. I traveled too much to have more lessons. Then I figured out that you will need English more than I need Russian."

I nod. It is a good thing that he only had two lessons. Why did they hug?

My husband continues, "I don't want you to turn out like Larissa."

"What do you mean? She seems fine to me. She has a fancy apartment, a job, pistachio ice cream, and a rude daughter."

I hope I will never have to visit her again. My husband doesn't need more Russian lessons. I can teach him all the Russian he wants.

My husband repeats, "I don't want you to be like Larissa, stuck between two countries."

"Do you want me to forget my motherland?"

"Not forget. But to give America a chance. To embrace a new culture and perfect the language, you must immerse yourself into your new life. If you keep watching Russian TV, surrounding yourself with Russian trinkets and books, you won't have time to learn new customs and speak good language."

"I went to ESL school for two months to study English."

"Yes. But you speak Russian to Sergey, and you don't have any friends outside the family because you can't carry a good conversation in English."

"It's unfair. I speak English."

"Not enough to get around without me."

I sniffle. I'm on the edge of tears, but I feel that this conversation is important, and I hold back.

"Inna, darling, listen," he says. "I'm not telling you to leave your old life and country behind and never speak of it again. I'm asking you to give America a chance. Try to learn more about everything around you—to speak, read, and write in English. Your Russian roots will always be with you, but today is your chance to accept the life you chose when we got married."

I sniffle again.

"You saw Larissa. She's made her home a shrine to Russia. She watches Russian TV and listens to Russian radio. She speaks Russian to her daughter and has poor grammar, even after ten years in the States. She couldn't find a decent job except as a store clerk because of her limited conversation skills. But her daughter is already making all the right choices—going to college, hanging out with native speakers, reading, and studying in English."

"I'm not as young as Sergey or Larissa's daughter."

"Inna, my dear wife, you are capable of doing anything you want. Just make it your goal. I will help you. I'm always here for you, but I'll be traveling again for business, and you will need to go around by yourself—drive to college, meet different people, and eventually find a job. You can do it. You are brave and smart. Don't give up."

I search for the tissues in my purse, but the hot tears don't wait for me to find the soft aloe vera case.

AUGUST-SEPTEMBER 2003

There is no manual at the library for how to become an American, but that Saturday visit to Larissa's swimming pool changed my degree of perseverance and my daily routine.

I passed the driving test. Now, when my husband travels, I drive with Sergey to Albertson's to get pistachio ice cream and to the library to get books in English for Sergey. I get my first English book, *The Day No Pigs Would Die*, by R.N. Peck. I read the book, keeping the dictionary next to me and writing all the unknown words into a notebook. It is a slow process.

I don't watch Russian channels or Russian YouTube videos anymore.

At home, Sergey and I only speak in English to each other. We go to church or take piano lessons from our neighbor Elizabeth— all in English, expanding our vocabulary and friend circles. Church activity opens a new realm for me. From canning to scrap-booking, the hobby opportunities are endless.

The new school year starts in the middle of August. It is so weird; all schools and colleges in Russia start on September first. I load my textbooks into a bag with my husband's company's logo and drive the old-fashioned Chevrolet Cutlass to the train station. The ESL school is located at 3300 South; it takes me 40 minutes by train and another twenty minutes by bus to get there. I go there every day, and I'm in the advanced class now.

Sergey is excited about middle school and taking a school bus. His English is really good, and he corrects my pronunciation and word choice. He grasps the language through games with his friends from school and neighborhood and youth activities. He reads all the available Harry Potter books over and over. He gets a beaten-up skateboard from a friend and practices outside for hours. Looking at his new summer spiky haircut and AC/DC T-shirt, sun-tanned face, and scraped knees, I would never have guessed this boy had lived anywhere else but America.

The food is another story. My Russian culinary degree in public catering and years of working in the restaurant seem to fail every time I try to cook something unfamiliar.

When my husband asks me about the food, I want to explain to him how Russian produce is "full of taste," grown without chemicals and pesticides, always fresh from local markets. But I don't have enough vocabulary to do it yet, so I simply say, "It is not yummy."

He has traveled the world and tried so many different cuisines and meals, but he is a diehard American and loves everything about it, including tasteless fast food.

My husband's oldest daughter, Janette, gives me a four-quart crock pot. For the next two weeks, our house smells like beef stew or chicken noodle soup, depending on the day of the week.

I try recipes from Japanese and Mexican cuisines. I can't say I've mastered them. Some turn out successful, and some—well, not edible.

On Labor Day weekend, Sergey leaves for Idaho for a couple of days with his friend to ride four-wheelers and go fishing. My husband is returning from his business trip to Seattle. I wake up alone and realize that I don't want to do anything. I don't even want to drive to get pistachio ice cream. I don't want to finish my book *The Day No Pigs Would Die.* I don't want to change from my pajamas or put on makeup.

Suddenly, I'm so homesick in that big empty house and would

give anything to be back in my tiny room with a common bathroom in the hostel where I lived with Sergey for six years. There, I
spoke, sang, read, and cracked jokes in Russian. I cooked Russian
food and didn't know how blessed I had been there in humble
circumstances and modest living, having friends and delicious
meals. I miss everything. I miss my family, my mom, my sister,
and my friends. And I miss the food.

I want to call my mom, but I exceeded the money limit on my
Noble phone card. I can send an email, but I decide to lie down
and cry. Will America ever feel like home?

Paul comes back from Seattle and finds me still in bed at 3:00 PM
My eyes are red, and my hair is a mess. He makes sure I'm not
sick and no one died. After our short conversation and my refusal
to leave the bed, I hear him talking on the phone with Laila. He
leaves, telling me he will be back with Laila.

By the time Paul returns with Laila, I have moved to the floor,
and rolled up in a ball in the corner behind the dresser. I hear
Paul's gentle voice.

"Hi, sweetheart. See what Laila and I got you."

I hear the rustle of plastic bags.

"What is it?" my voice comes hoarse.

"Scrapbooking supplies. I hope you'll like it. It's for creating
pages of happy memories. You take pictures."

A long howl escapes my throat, interrupting Paul's explanations.

"I don't have any happy memories," I cry out. "I have no
friends. I spent this summer alone, reading stupid English books
with no sense. I miss my mom, and I want to go back to Russia."

Paul and Laila sit on the floor where I curl up in my pink pajamas. Paul takes my hand in his. I pull back. He puts his hand on
my shoulder. His soft voice always consoles Laila and Sergey

when they scrape a knee or get in a quarrel with each other. I only hope that he feels what I feel and finds the right words for me too. If we go back to Russia, Paul will be so sad. I know that Sergey wouldn't want to go back. He doesn't miss our small apartment with no bathroom where we lived in Russia. I can only imagine what Paul is feeling right now. I know I'm breaking his heart. He told me he cannot go through another divorce. But at this moment, I'm homesick, miserable, and selfish.

After a pause, Paul's soft voice carries over.

"Inna, darling, being nostalgic is okay. You lived in Russia for thirty-five years, and you've been in America for only six months. There will be times when we'll go to Russia and visit your family. And they will come here to visit America, too."

Now, I grab Paul's hand. He continues.

"We love you and Sergey. You are both part of our family now. I want you to be happy and have a happy life here with us, with me. Please, don't cry. You will have friends because you have a good heart, and you are a very sociable person. Just give it time."

My voice comes out muffled. "But I miss my home and Russian stuff."

"Stuff like what?" asks Paul.

"Like my mom, aunt, sister, cats, and food."

"Cats?" Paul's voice is surprised.

"Well, I can't bring any of your family members here right away. But we can talk with the landlord about having a cat. But for food—you are the best cook. You can cook your Russian food anytime you want. There is a Russian store on 4500 South. We can go there and buy some Russian produce. And you can cook whatever you want. We call that 'comfort food.' Why don't we try that?"

I lift my puffy face and swipe my shaggy hair away.

"Russian store? Why didn't you tell me before? Can I cook Russian food? And you won't be mad?"

Paul shrugs his shoulders, looks at his daughter, and smiles.

"Why would I be mad?"

"Well, you said you don't want our home to look like Larissa's little Russia."

"You can cook your Russian food anytime you want. I'm sure everyone will love it."

SEPTEMBER 2003

The Russian store feels like stepping back in time. Familiar food names and brands, cheeses, sausages, spices, nuts, deli meats, and an overwhelming variety of sweets. Food that my American family would never appreciate or love as I do—sardines, herrings, dry fish, halva, and hard gingerbread cookies. We buy four bags of food. Also, we buy some vegetables. I know that the cabbage and dill were grown and harvested here, on American soil, but the fact that the produce is sold in the Russian store somehow makes it fresher.

I'm cooking borscht and piroshki with potatoes today. It takes me several hours to get everything ready by the time Laila and Sergey come back from school. Sergey yells that he is not hungry but grabs a couple of piroshki and runs outside to play with his friends.

Laila goes to her bedroom and comes back to the kitchen table, where I serve her dinner. We bless the food, and I offer Laila a bit of sour cream for her borscht. She shakes her head. It's a Russian thing—borscht with sour cream and piroshki instead of bread. Maybe one day she will try it.

My heart skips a bit when Laila takes her first spoonful to her mouth. I want her to like it. I want her to know that I'm trying really hard to adjust to this life. I want to share my culture and the food that represents it.

Laila swallows the soup, nods, and takes a bite of piroshki. I'm grateful that she doesn't spit it into her napkin. She keeps eating, blowing on her spoon. I think she likes it. I sigh in relief and pick up my spoon.

My Russian borscht is salty, sweet, spicy, hot, tangy, and rich to the taste. It is not the same soup that my grandma would cook on her wood-burning stove. It has its own smell and taste. I enjoy every bite.

My American home smells like Russian borscht today. It is a different smell. It is a different taste. But it is good. I think I will like it here.

ABOUT THE AUTHORS

C.W. Allen is a Midwestern transplant to rural Utah where she serves as the President-Elect of the League of Utah Writers. She writes long stories for children and short stories for former children. She is also a frequent guest presenter at writing conferences, which helps her procrastinate knuckling down to any actual writing. Her award-winning middle grade fantasy series *The Falinnheim Chronicles* is out now, with many more stories waiting in the wings. Follow her latest projects at cwallenbooks.com.

Eric John Anderson (He/Him) is an award-winning author and screenwriter from Utah. He has lived on both American coasts, but finds peace when lost deep in the mountain wilderness. When he's not writing queer literary fiction or supernatural horror, he's playing intense strategy board games or explaining obscure films to his uninterested friends. His work can be found in the upcoming anthologies *Twisted Tales* and *No Exit*.

Sheena Blankenagel resides in southern Utah and enjoys taking her laptop into the red rock desert to write. She's received recognition in contests such as L. Ron Hubbard's Writers of the Future, the Utah Original Writing Competition, and the Olive Woolley Burt Awards, and is currently writing a fantasy trilogy centered around Greek mythology. When away from the keyboard, Sheena scoops her family up for outdoor adventures like camping, hiking, and soaking in hot springs.

Carolyn Campbell is the author of three nationally-published books and 900 magazine articles, many of them in national magazines.

Timothy Doyle retired from his position as a physics professor at Utah Valley University in 2018. He has worked as a scientist for over 40 years in such diverse fields as earthquake science, nuclear reactor safety, developing methods to inspect the Space Shuttle Solid Rocket Boosters, and detection of residual cancer in tissue during breast cancer surgery. This is the first publication of a poem of his in a book.

Gina G. grew up in southern Utah, where the summer sun spends the winter. She managed to get away and escape to Washington State, where she lived for twenty-three years. She fell in love with the tall evergreen trees, the mountains, the city of Seattle, and the rain. Life and circumstances brought her back to her hometown. She is the author of the LGBTQ erotic series *Secrets Cafe* and has published short stories in several anthologies. She is a League of Utah Writers member, the Write On Chapter, and Infinite Monkeys. Her short story, "Culling The Humans," won a Quills Bronze Typewriter award in 2023. She spends her days selling shoes and her nights writing under the watchful eye of her curious black cat, Fish. Every day she misses the rain.

Joseph (Joe) Gordon is an award winning author, speaker, and educator and brings almost fifty years of business/educational/technical writing experience to the creative process. Based on this background, he claims his creative process is "organized chaos". In terms of relevant experience for the mystery/thriller/spy stories he writes, Joe worked as a police officer, both as a patrolman and an evidence specialist. He also spent time in the US Army Security Agency doing intelligence work, including tours of duty in Viet Nam and at the National Security Agency. He is a retired college educator and has degrees from

Arizona State and Utah State and frequently presents and does training on a variety of writing and communication topics.

Johanna Greenberg was born in Boston, MA. She spent her formative teenage years in New Jersey, which allowed for sneaking into the jungle of New York City, where the seeds of her creative soul were planted. She received her bachelor's degree in English with a focus on creative writing from the University of Washington in 2000 and has been writing poetry and short stories ever since. She has travelled and lived all over the West, exploring mountains, defying death, and meeting the most interesting people along the way. She is the mother of two incredible boys who she credits with inspiring persistent curiosity and wonder about the world around her. She is based in Salt Lake City, UT and works in healthcare. Her writing is currently focused on poetry, short story, and spoken storytelling. She explores themes related to the landscape of the Mountain West, the complexity of the human experience, and mysteries of our universe. In 2024, she received the literary arts prize from the Alfred Lambourne Program and the Gold Typewriter in Flash Fiction from the League of Utah Writers. She is currently working on a collection of short stories and a novel. She self-publishes her work on the Substack platform.

Josie Hume has a BA in Creative Writing from Weber State. A regular winner in the Olive Woolley Burt Awards, she has published a variety of short fiction, creative non-fiction and poetry and has written several novels. Josie is a wife and mother, a disabled veteran, and amateur builder. She lives in Utah where she spends her time writing, reading, and in the company of loving family and friends. Life is good. You can read more of her work at her rarely-updated website: josiehume.com.

L.S. Kunz lives in northern Utah with her husband. She is a member of the League of Utah Writers and has received local awards for her short stories and middle grade fiction. Her work has appeared in *Ellery Queen Mystery Magazine*, *Baubles From Bones*, *The Last Line*, *Winter Horrorland: An Undertaker Books Anthology*, and *Utah's Best Poetry & Prose 2023*.

C. H. Lindsay (Charlie) is an award-winning poet & writer, housewife, and book-lover—not necessarily in that order. She currently has short stories and poems in over forty anthologies and magazines including *Amazing Stories, Fantasy Magazine, Moonletters, Space and Time Magazine, Strange Horizons,* and *Utah's Best Poetry & Prose*. She is currently working on five novels, six short stories, and at least two dozen poems (although the numbers are always in flux). In 2018 she became Al Carlisle's literary executor. She now publishes his true crime under Carlisle Legacy Books, LLC. She is a member of SFWA, HWA, SFPA, LUW, and is a founding member of the Utah Chapter of the Horror Writers Association. Mostly blind, she lives in Utah with her "seeing-eye husband," library of books, and a bossy cat. You can learn more about her at www.chlindsay.net.

Inna Valerie Lyon is a Russian bumpkin raised on a steady diet of cabbage and potatoes peppered with the required reading of Chekhov and Dostoevsky. During the day, Inna works as an accountant and specializes in producing colorful aging reports and cute collection letters. At night, she writes stories about life, miracles, and cats. Inna is a member of the League of Utah Writers, the Infinite Monkeys, and currently serves as president of the Blue Quill chapter. She is an award-winning writer in different genres. She writes in both languages, English and Russian. And she loves to see her readers laugh or cry, or at least, remember her story for the next fifteen minutes….

Pat Partridge writes across genres. He is the author of the mystery, *Fragile Memories*, the sequel, *Buried at Bears Ears*, and the humorous road-trip novel *Fast on Fifty.* His book of political humor is now in its third edition. Over the past three years he has won eleven awards from the League of Utah Writers for his short fiction and novel first chapters. His story, "The New Dress," which first appeared in *LitroUK*, received the Emerald Award for best short work across all categories. His short fiction has appeared in *Remington Review, The Haven, Fabula Argentea, Ariel Chart, Litro,* and multiple anthologies. He is pleased others find his writing worth reading.

Michael Shoemaker is a poet and photographer from Magna. Utah. He is the author of three poetry/photography collections, is a three-time nominee for the 2025 Best of the Net Anthology Awards and his poetry will appear in *Boundless 2024: The Anthology of the Rio Grande Valley International Poetry Festival.*

Linda F. Smith practiced law in Boston for eight years before moving to Utah to be a professor at the University of Utah S J Quinney College of Law where she oversaw the internship program. Since retirement she has tried to correct injustices through her fiction such as "The Ham Sandwich." She is grateful to her former students and their supervising attorneys for sharing their challenges in representing the disenfranchised. Linda also continues to do volunteer legal work in the family law area and legal advocacy in a variety of venues--where ever windmills need tilting at. In her spare time she goes to circuit training and indoor cycling with her husband and younger son, cheers on her two grandchildren in their sports, and compares NY Times puzzle answers with her other son and daughter-in-law.

Mae Thorn enjoys being romanced and terrified- a combination not normally found in books so she writes them. Her favorite stories include kickass women and the men they fall for. She writes historical romance, fantasy, and horror. She has published three historical romance books: *Notorious, Dangerous,* and *Rebellious.* Mae holds a Bachelor's degree in English from the University of Utah and a Master's degree in Library and Information Science from San Jose State University. She is the co-president of the League of Utah Writers Romance Chapter, and she lives near Salt Lake City, Utah with her cats; Church, Shadow Moon, and Sabrina, and a puppy, Whiskey.

Marie Tollstrup hails from a Wisconsin potato farm. In 1951 at fourteen, she entered a convent, the School Sisters of St. Francis, in Milwaukee. After graduating from Alverno College with a BA in English, she taught as a nun for ten years in Schiller Park and Wilmette in the Chicago area where she earned an MA in English from Loyola University. At Jordan High School in Long Beach, California, where she taught twenty-nine years, she founded and advised Stylus, a national award-winning literary arts magazine for twenty-three years. In retirement, Marie focuses on poetry, but branches out to prose where she enters contests, winning awards for speaking her mind and poetic word play. Her poetry has been published in UTSPS's *Panorama* for ten years, in twelve League of Utah Writers' volumes, and her chapbook, *Starspun*, published by Moon in the Rye Press. Read her published poems and prose in LUW's publications.

Thomas I. Wahl is a Quills award-winning author. Following his retirement, he has dedicated himself to creative writing, specializing in short stories and historical fiction informed by his agricultural experiences in Northwest Iowa and his family history. Wahl and his wife live in Salt Lake City, where he enjoys photography, brewing beer, making BBQ sauces/rubs, and dog treats.

Kalie Walker is a UX Writer and fantasy author. Her short story, "The Redbells of Winwich," recently won first place in the Olive Woolley Burt Awards, New Voices category. She lives with her partner of seven years and her three (yes, three) cats in Vineyard, Utah.

"When excavating family history, certain circumstances come to the surface, and that is the gift of our ancestors to their descendants." **Julie Walton** has been writing short stories since her young adulthood specializing in the "skeletons in the family closet." Bringing light to the situation can help us have more understanding and maybe empathy. Her technical writing for a local newspaper and TV station helped Julie hone her storytelling skills, in addition to supporting her family. Julie has lived in Southern Utah for over 25 years and loves the mountains, but loves the desert too.

Johnny Worthen is an award-winning, best-selling author of books and stories. Trained in stand-up comedy, modern literary criticism and cultural studies, he writes excellent multi-genre fiction, symbolized by his love of tie-dye and good words. "I wear tie-dye for my friends, but I write what I like to read," he says. "This guarantees me at least one fan and easy dressing decisions in the morning." Johnny's best-selling series, The BOOKS OF CORONAM, is an epic science fiction series in the vein of Frank Herbert's DUNE. It is available from Flame Tree Press, with international distribution through Simon and Schuster. Johnny's newest book, THE GAIA CHIME, has been called a "cli-fi horror." It follows the lives of two filmmakers who witness the ancient echo of drastic and terrible renewal. Johnny teaches writing at the University of Utah and lives in a house with his wife, sons and assorted cats. There's also a lawn.

D.J. Wray is a mother, grandmother, lover of Nature, and walks where only the whisper of the wind and the sound of her own voice can be heard. (She likes to talk out loud to herself all the time. Sometimes her plants also benefit from these conversations.) D.J. loves to work with stained glass, and has a number of handmade windows in her house that provide endless variations of colored patterns on the wall as the light shifts outside. She loves walking through hardware stores and thinking about what she might be able to make from all the washers, pipes and wood. The 'thinking about it' part is key, because she's usually too busy trying to keep up with her writing goals, and working at other jobs to keep a roof over her head. But as long as she can wake up each day with health and all the possibilities that lay ahead in a day, life is good.

Susan J. Wurtzburg has won or placed in several poetry competitions. She is a Commissioned Artist in *Sidewalk Poetry: Senses of Salt Lake City, 2024*, and an Associate Poetry Editor at *Poets Reading the News.* Her book, *Ravenous Words,* with Lisa Lucas will appear in spring, 2025. Webpage: susanwurtzburg.com

Laurel Yeates has been writing about her life since she was a young girl, following in the footsteps of her parents, her grandmother and her daughter, who was first published at age 12. Now a grandmother retired from a career in journalism and teaching, she is delighted to share one of the most important essays she's written, a piece that speaks to the unique and loving relationship she had with her grandmother. She lives in Salt Lake City with John, her husband of 49 years. They have daughters and grandchildren who live in Minneapolis and Seattle.

Bryan Young (he/they) works across many different media. His work as a writer and producer has been called "filmmaking gold" by The New York Times. He's also published comic books with Slave Labor Graphics and Image Comics. He's been a regular contributor for the *Huffington Post, StarWars.com, Star Wars Insider magazine, SYFY, /Film,* and was the founder and editor in chief of the geek news and review site *Big Shiny Robot!* In 2014, he wrote the critically acclaimed history book, *A Children's Illustrated History of Presidential Assassination.* He co-authored *Robotech: The Macross Saga RPG* and has written five books in the BattleTech Universe: *Honor's Gauntlet, A Question of Survival, Fox Tales, Without Question*, and *VoidBreaker.* His latest non-fiction tie-in book, *The Big Bang Theory Book of Lists* is a #1 Bestseller on Amazon. His work has won two Diamond Quill awards and in 2023 he was named Writer of the Year by the League of Utah Writers. He teaches writing for *Writer's Digest, Script Magazine,* and at the University of Utah. Follow him across social media @swankmotron or visit swankmotron.com.

MORE FROM THE LEAGUE OF UTAH WRITERS

FIND ALL OUR ANTHOLOGIES AT LEAGUEOFUTAHWRITERS.COM

THE LEAGUE OF UTAH WRITERS
2022 ANTHOLOGY

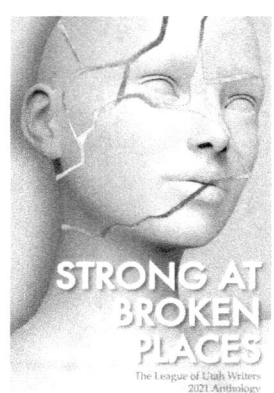

STRONG AT
BROKEN
PLACES

The League of Utah Writers
2021 Anthology

WHAT CAN THE LEAGUE OF UTAH WRITERS DO FOR YOU?

The League of Utah Writers is a non-profit organization dedicated to offering friendship, education, and encouragement to the writers and poets of Utah. Our organization aids our members in the improvement of their craft and support of their goals.

The League of Utah Writers is a vibrant writing community with chapters throughout the state, as well as online with members across the country. Membership in the League of Utah Writers provides support and opportunities for writers and editors at all levels of their careers.

Join us at www.leagueofutahwriters.com

The
Pre-Quill
Conference

Pre-Quill is the League of Utah Writers' Spring writing conference - a day long event of classes, workshops, and networking with other wordsmiths.

This event showcases our local Utah writers in classes and courses geared to each unique voice and talent. It is also a great place to start working on stories, poetry, or any of the other categories listed in the Wooley awards - the League's prestigious contest awarded at the annual Quills conference each year.

Pre-Quill helps refresh your creative neurons with the pulse and energy only spring could bring.

Find more about The Pre-Quill Conference at
www.leagueofutahwriters.com

The League of Utah Writers invites you to join us for the Quills Conference, hosted locally in Salt Lake City annually near the end of summer.

The Quills Conference is the League's premium event, bringing in special guest authors, agents, editors, and publishers from around the nation.

This four-day writing conference is for everyone from the fresh voices not yet published to the well-established writers seeking to make a difference in their writing community.

The Quills Conference's annual banquet is also home to The Woolley Awards writing contest and the Quill Awards for published works.

Find out more about Quills at
www.leagueofutahwriters.com